THE
DON CARLOS

DANIEL BRENTS

outskirts
press

Outskirts Press, Inc.
http://www.outskirtspress.com

ISBN: 978-1-9772-5956-1

Outskirts Press and the "OP" logo are trademarks belonging to Outskirts Press, Inc.

PRINTED IN THE UNITED STATES OF AMERICA

With thanks to Betty, Barry, and Tom for your love and support

*With gratitude to Nancy, Ron, and Maria for your
help in finding more of the puzzle pieces*

With sympathy for those affected by these events

With apologies to those whose parts were fictionalized

SUNDAY, JUNE 3, 1945, 7:32 P.M.
CENTRAL WAR TIME—DALLAS, TEXAS

Sunday had been uncomfortably warm. The afternoon had passed as usual in early summer. Visits had been exchanged between relatives and friends; children splashed each other with water hoses; and adults washed their cars, baked pies in the kitchen, or read a favorite book.

The house at 3516 Rosedale Boulevard was an exception; there were no children playing, and no one was washing the car or reading a book or preparing dinner. Earlier on Sunday morning, a young woman, stylishly dressed wearing a hat and gloves, left the house alone after firmly closing and locking the front door. She did not return until four o'clock, still alone, and then only stayed only a few minutes before she reemerged, turned left, and walked quickly east down the sidewalk. There was no other sign of movement along the block as she walked. Hours passed, and as the sun began to fade, shadows lengthened and twilight fell. It was time for most families in the suburban neighborhood to clean the dishes after dinner and put the silverware away. The streets were completely still as darkness grew.

Suddenly, a cold white light flashed, and a shot rang out through the open kitchen window of the Rosedale house. Black clouds of starlings erupted from the trees, swirling and wheeling, and the warm air was dense with the sound of their flight, like damp sheets flapping in a night breeze. As they settled again, the sound of their wings and raucous calls faded into the dim shadows, and silence fell over the neighborhood once again.

CHAPTER ONE

SUNDAY, JUNE 3, 1945, 8:25 P.M. CWT—DALLAS

Doris had returned to the house on Rosedale. She called the police and nervously prepared herself for the knock on the door. Once she heard it, she rose, smoothed her skirt, crossed the living room to the tiled foyer, turned on the porch light, and opened the door. Two men stood outside and identified themselves as police officers. The larger heavyset man dressed in plainclothes asked if she was Mrs. Benson. "Yes, I am," she said, confirming that it was she who had called the police. "Please come in, Officers." June bugs, attracted by the porch light, were drunkenly attacking the screen door, so she closed it quickly again as the men removed their hats and stepped inside.

The larger man said, "Thank you, ma'am. I'm Detective Barnett, and this is Sergeant Farrow. We're here in response to your call." Barnett was nearly bald, and Sergeant Farrow, the accompanying policeman who was in uniform, was smaller and comparatively wiry in build.

"Please follow me," she said as she led them across the foyer and through the kitchen to the breakfast room. She stood aside, shuddering anew at the sight of the body and the gore in the small breakfast area, the odors of blood, tissue, gun smoke, body fluids, and liquor, rancid in the still air. Even as she steeled herself for it, the scene took her breath away.

She crossed her forearms, fidgeting with her handkerchief, and answered the detective's questions as he walked counterclockwise around the breakfast table, moving carefully so as not to disturb the evidence. He noted the swiveled chair, the sprawled corpse lying head down on the table, the still pool of blood, and brain tissue spattered everywhere about the opposite wall. He leaned over and inspected the pistol lying near the body's outstretched right hand. "Is this how you found him?" asked the detective.

"Yes, when I came in, I saw this and knew he was dead," said Doris. Then turning at the sound of a second, insistent knock at the front of the house, Doris excused herself and returned to the foyer to see behind the screen door a small, intense man in his mid-forties, wearing wire-rimmed glasses, a rumpled suit, a battered gray hat, and a crooked tie. He held a half-chewed cigar in his mouth and carried a worn leather briefcase. A tall, middle-aged woman with permed hair stood behind him, also carrying a case. "Mrs. Benson?" the man asked as he pulled the screen door open and stepped inside, hardly waiting for her reply. He had seen the police car when he arrived, so he was sure this was the right place.

"Y-yes, that's right," she said a little surprised. She hadn't expected so many people.

She confirmed details about Carlos, the victim, such as his name, Don Carlos, the date and place of his birth, his parents, and his current employer. Doris told him that his recent employer was an auto parts distributor, and that Carlos managed their sales across a several states. After Doris affirmed her name, the man introduced himself. She was a bit put off by the gruff manner of the man, but she stood her ground.

"I'm Lew Sterrett, the Dallas County justice of the peace," he said, "and I'll be serving as the coroner in this case."

"Are you a doctor?" Doris asked.

"No, ma'am, we only need a medical examiner when the death is a result of natural causes. Now, can you to take me to the scene?"

She gestured to the kitchen in reply to his query. She followed only as far as the doorway to the kitchen as the JP and lead detective began talking. The woman who had accompanied the justice remained in the entry way, standing very still.

The detective in charge looked up and beckoned to Doris. "What time did the shooting occur, ma'am?"

Doris replied, "I don't know; I was away with a friend while it happened. It must have been between the time that I left, at about 4:30, and 8:00 when I returned." Glancing at the overturned whiskey bottle and glass, she confirmed that her husband, Carlos, had been drinking that day, ever since the morning as she left for church. The detective, whose large form obscured the pistol in shadow, grasped the gun and straightened, his knees creaking from the effort.

Justice Sterrett looked up from his notes and asked Doris, "So you were not present in the house when this happened?"

"No, sir," said Doris.

"That's funny," said Sterrett. "The dispatcher said you told her that were at home when the...er, death occurred."

"She must have misunderstood," said Doris. "I called the police just as soon as I came in and saw what happened."

The justice was making notes and asked a few more questions about her activities that day. After checking the weapon, a .38 caliber, the policeman placed it in a paper bag, marking the bag with identifying information. He then went to the side door, opened it, and looked outside. As wave of cricket chirps poured in, he closed it.

Sterrett asked her to accompany him to the dining parlor and be seated, to answer some more questions about the evening's events and the deceased. They took chairs across the table from one another. The tall woman who came with Sterrett sat down next to him, opened her typewriter case, and rolled sheets of paper and carbons, while the justice took out a pad of writing paper and a block of forms. He began to ask Doris questions about Carlos, his background, particulars, and about her movements during the day, while the stenographer typed a record of the discussion.

Doris told him about his drinking that day and her movements.

She said she left the house at about 4:30 p.m. to go to a movie downtown with a friend. The show was over about 6:45 p.m., but she said she did not return immediately; she window shopped before coming home at about 8:00 p.m. When she opened the door, she said she smelled something strange, so she called out for Carlos, but there was no answer. She went back to the kitchen where there was a light on.

"As I came to the kitchen doorway, the smells grew very strong. I stepped through and saw him slumped over the breakfast table, the gun near his right hand, and there was blood just everywhere! There was so much, and there was this terrible smell of gun smoke and whiskey where the bottle had fallen over, and it was horrible, it...

"I walked to the right side of the table, but I could see he was dead...there was no...he couldn't have"—she sobbed, then resumed—"he had knocked over the bottle of whiskey...I screamed, I think, and then I came out to the hallway and called the police."

The coroner asked her why the back door was unlocked, although she had earlier said all the doors were locked. She said he must have unlocked it while she was away.

"Now I want you to think, does anyone else have access to the house, or a key to any of the doors—a maid maybe, a friend, a neighbor, or a family member?"

"No," she said, "no one else has a key. We only have one spare, and we keep it in the garden near the back door."

She said he had been feeling bad lately about his job situation, but he seemed to be looking forward to things improving now that the war was turning our way—he said he was optimistic that things would get better.

The coroner asked if they had any money problems, or if he had problems at work, and she replied that things were tight, but they were keeping their heads above water and that he liked the people at work—he liked everybody. She said they all liked him.

"It's just that the car business has been tough lately, with the war cutting production and people holding on to their old jalopies. But he thought it would turn around."

The coroner asked if he had been drinking a lot lately, and she said, "No more than usual, no more than anybody, I guess."

In answer to his next question, she said that she rarely drank at all.

Then the justice asked, "Were things all right between the two of you?" She answered that things between them were fine. They recently had their anniversary, and he had told her that he was happier than he had ever been.

The justice asked her if she had any preference of a local funeral home to take charge of the remains. She said she didn't, and he offered to call one for her. She said the funeral service would be in Oklahoma, which reminded her to call his mother once he finished with the telephone.

As Doris described her day, the justice mentally sorted through the checklist of evidence. "Mrs. Benson," he said, "we're going to keep this case open for a while and classify it for the present as 'a presumed suicide.'"

When the interview was complete, the justice thanked her, asked if he could use her telephone, and went back into the kitchen to make a call and consult with the policemen, while the stenographer finished typing her notes and completed a Certificate of Death.

Before long, there was another knock at the door. Doris got up and answered it. A representative from the funeral home and two assistants were outside and explained that the coroner had called them. She showed them into the crowded breakfast room, and the funeral home representative asked them to make room so they could begin the removal process. In response to their request, Doris went to the bedroom and gathered some of his clothing, putting the items in a cardboard box that they gave her—a suit, tie, shirt, some stockings, a belt, and a pair of shoes. Then she brought the box to the living room where the funeral director wrote on the box "Personal Effects: DOD 6/3/45" and the victim's name scrawled upon it. As they carried the corpse out into the night on a rubber stretcher under a heavy canvas cover, she sat back down at the dining room table, where the justice was reviewing the death certificate.

"Mrs. Benson, please read this over and confirm the details with your signature."

Doris was tired but calm now. When the two policemen, justice of the peace, and stenographer departed, it was just after 10:30 p.m.

CHAPTER TWO

JUNE 4, 1945, 10:15 A.M.
—DALLAS COUNTY COURTHOUSE

The next morning, Sterrett was reviewing the case with Detective Barnett. "I don't know," the justice said. "There are some things that don't quite add up to me. For starters, what's up with his handle, Don Carlos, like a mobster or a Spanish grandee? Where was she really at the time when the guy died? There were other things too. She said everything was hunky-dory between them, but then she also said she was so upset with his drinking that she left the house. Then also, the way she was dressed, like a fashion plate, and that house, but how did they afford it? The guy had just started work as an auto parts salesman and she's a secretary."

The detective added, "Yeah, I know. Our dispatcher says the wife definitely told her that she was at home when it happened. Also, there was that funny business with the back door being unlocked when she said they always kept it locked."

Sterrett concluded, "There are enough inconsistencies for me to keep it open a while longer. Let's just see if we can learn a little bit more, maybe talk to their upstairs tenant and some neighbors."

However, as often happens with cold cases, Sterrett and the detective soon both had other pressing matters, and with no one actively pursuing the case, the file drifted steadily downward in the pile on their desks.

CHAPTER THREE

1897 TO 1916—GROWING UP IN INDIAN TERRITORY

Carlos Benson, his birth name, was born in Indian Territory, which is now part of Oklahoma and was admitted into the Union as a state in 1907. Before that, it was known as the "Twin Territories," consisting of the eastern "Indian Territory," to which tribes of Indians from the southern and western US had been summarily relocated, and "Oklahoma Territory" in the west, which was mostly inhabited by white immigrants from the southern US. The roughly equal halves in size were overseen by the US government. In Indian Territory, white settlers lived alongside areas reserved for the "Five Civilized Tribes" (Cherokee, Choctaw, Chickasaw, Creek, and Seminole), condescendingly so designated by government officials of the time. The tribes were governed by a white representative appointed by the president of the United States. It would not be until 1970 that congress would pass a law permitting the five tribes to elect their own leaders and govern themselves.

The population was sparse, and in Indian Territory, the economy was 70 percent agricultural and impoverished. Other economic sectors were slowly growing, such as rail construction, natural resources development, and institutional employment. Less than forty years before, the Civil War had upended the economy in the southern states, which was previously dependent upon slavery. Many who had fought for the Confederacy were left unemployed, displaced, homeless, and resentful. Carlos's grandfather was one of these, although he accepted his fate. The South had always been his home, and although he had no particular interest in slavery, he had fought for the South, was wounded at Chickamauga, and afterward went to medical school in Macon, Georgia. Denied a pension by the US government, he relied on the practice of surgery until his palsy condition became so bad that he was forced to stop and take up pharmacy instead. These areas were a refuge for the vanquished who sought land and opportunity, and for displaced natives with little or no formal education or social services. The lax regulation and enforcement created a magnet for malcontents who had little regard for law, order, or the social compact.

Such were the conditions when Carlos was born in 1897 in Wynnewood, Indian Territory. Oddly, in the future he would randomly place his birth year as 1898. His father and grandfather ran a pharmacy there. Carlos was named after Carlos Montezuma, the first male Native American to earn a medical degree from an American university, who was revered by both Carlos's grandfather and his mother, who was part Cherokee. It was their hope that Carlos would someday also enter the medical profession. The family soon relocated to Ada, another nearby small rural community, where there was no electricity, no sidewalks, poor sanitation, and the unpaved, muddy, or dusty streets smelled of horse droppings and the occasional desiccated domestic animal. Education was rudimentary. In this place and time, there were no conveniences that we now take for granted—no air conditioning or central heat, no automobiles or airplanes, no grocery stores as we know them, no refrigerators, or kitchen appliances. The few telephones in use were only in Oklahoma City, nearly ninety miles away. Long-distance travel was by horseback, wagon, or railroad, and the nearest rail station was several hours from such a rural outpost until a spur line was run from Tulsa. Clothing was typically homemade from dry goods, if not homespun, and only occasionally washed. There would be no radio until 1922, and then only within range of Oklahoma City.

Doctors were in short supply, and like Carlos's grandfather, Thomas Elias Benson, they traveled a circuit on horseback to visit their patients, who were treated with the few medicines that could be carried in the physician's saddlebags. The odors arising from an open medical saddlebag were both nauseating and unforgettable, including fumes from sulfur, arsenic, mercury, iodine, quinoline, or various ground herbs and minerals. Cough syrups routinely contained opium, and cocaine was used to treat headaches. Victims of serious accidents or illnesses often died before they could receive any medical attention, or they might die because they received it. The life expectancy for men was just over forty-six years, and for women just over forty-eight years. The mortality rate for children aged one to four was 19.8 per thousand nationally but was much higher in remote communities such as this. Children wore "asphidity bags," which were foul-smelling bags of pungent herbs, to ward off disease, and they wore "union suits" (long, one-piece undergarments) into which they were sewn for the entire winter. It took a healthy constitution and a full measure of luck to stay alive in such conditions.

Like hygiene, the law was only dimly understood and spotty in its application. With a relatively weak and decentralized administration, Indian Territory was one of the last frontiers of the Wild West, and the little community of Ada, in what was then the Chickasaw Nation, and where Carlos grew up, was one of the outlaws' last retreats.

One of these desperados, Jim "Deacon" Miller, had boasted of killing twenty-one people. Miller was contracted by local ranchers to kill a US Marshal for $1,700, and he succeeded. The Marshal was a Freemason, and a member of the local lodge. The law-abiding citizens were outraged, and soon after the killing, Miller and three others were captured and bound over to district court to wait for trial. In the early morning hours, a crowd of local men, thought to include and perhaps be led by Freemasons, broke into the jail, overpowered the deputy sheriff and the jailer, and lynched the four in a livery barn across an alley from the jail. The persons responsible for the lynching were never identified. It was obvious that the community and surrounding areas would benefit from a more reliable law enforcement presence.[1]

_____

[1] *The Early History of Ada*, J. Hugh Biles

CHAPTER 4

THE PEACE OFFICER

Carlos's father, Ed, having little formal education, was attracted to law enforcement. Upon the invitation and help of a fellow Mason who was a US Marshal, he sold his pharmacy and entered the Indian Service, first in 1898 as a Constable helping with administrative duties, and later in 1902 as a Deputy US Marshal involved in operations at the regional center in Muskogee, Indian Territory.

At first, the focus of his work was disrupting the flow of bootleg moonshine between outlaws and native Indians. Later, during Prohibition, he worked to interrupt the distribution of banned alcohol to the broader community. Known as a "Dry Raider," he was highly effective, and that meant he was on the trail and gone from home and family more often than not. Although it was sometimes dangerous work, from time to time the marshal would take one or two of his sons along with him on raids.

One sweltering afternoon, Marshal Ed, accompanied by young Carlos, was leading a posse back from a successful raid on a bootlegger's still outside of Henryetta, eighty miles from Ada and southwest of Muskogee. At a dusty little country store in Okmulgee, about midway back, the men stopped to buy cold drinks. As Ed walked into the dimly lit store, the proprietor reached under the counter in front of him and drew a pistol, aiming it straight at the Marshal. It seemed that just over a year previously, the Marshal had arrested the man's brother, who had been running a still outside of town.

His face clouded with rage, and the storekeeper shouted, "I keela you, I keela you!" He was of Italian extraction and was prone to overexcitement.

"Put the gun down, Baptiste," said Ed, with calm authority. "If there's any killing to be done here, I'm the one who's going to do it." After which, he turned his back on Baptiste and said, "Now, boys, what kind of pop do you want? I'm buying."

The storekeeper hesitated, then put the gun away and waited for drink orders. Carlos would never forget how his father had handled that situation, making his own luck by maintaining a cool head in the face of imminent danger.

CHAPTER FIVE

THE BENSON FAMILY

Raising a family in these uncertain conditions was extremely difficult, and it placed enormous demands on the women, as men and boys were usually needed to earn an income for the family. Families had to adjust to opportunities, and that often meant pulling up stakes and moving to seek new and better prospects.

Marshal Ed's wife, Susan, had chiseled features, dark hair and eyes, and a quiet demeanor. She had been born in Georgia to a father who was part Cherokee, and she, like her husband, was steady and calm as a rock. As a young mother, left to raise their five children almost single-handedly, she kept the household running with sweet humor, delegating duties, assigning chores, confiding in her daughters, managing her sons, taking in boarders, and making ends meet. Her faith kept her strong, and her children were her joy. As her husband was a third generation Master Mason in the Freemasons, she was a member of the Order of the Eastern Star, the women's affiliate organization. She was also a member of the Women's Christian Temperance Union. Both she and her husband were dedicated teetotalers.

Carlos was the middle son, the fourth child among five siblings. There was Lula Belle, the oldest, who would later marry, move just across the state line to Texas, go to California, divorce, and remarry to live as a rancher's wife in California's Imperial Valley, raising their only daughter, Lila June. Next was Maude, a sweet, amiable girl who later fell in love with Arch Pittman, bore his daughter, Marjorie, and raised her alone after Arch died of asphyxiation from a faulty gas space heater while traveling on business in the mid-1920s. The two sisters and their daughters would later come together during The Depression, living in Oklahoma City from Belle's husband's earnings from Chevrolet and Belle's seamstress work. Max was the oldest boy, who imitated his father's bravado but had little ability to extend himself with his father's purpose and dedication. The youngest was Ed, Jr., who inherited his father's name, Thomas Edward, to the smoldering resentment of Max, who felt he deserved it as the oldest son. Ed, Jr. was carefree, cheerful, and loved being with people.

CHAPTER SIX

BOYHOOD IN INDIAN TERRITORY

As often happens with middle children, and especially in large families, Carlos craved love, attention, and approval. He had a sunny disposition, and as was unusual for a young boy, was self-assured in his dealings with adults. He volunteered to do chores for his neighbors, such as raking the lawn for old Mrs. Jackson down the street or watering and currying Mr. Phillips's horse. Among his own age group, he was a joker and a playful prankster. One time he put a frog in Billy Jenkins's lunchbox and was rewarded by a yelp of surprise when Billy opened it. He was daring and always ready for a challenge, like the time he single-handedly beat back a blaze in the schoolhouse.

He was lucky, winning and outperforming at every challenge. While he was always cheerful, that good cheer arose from his bravado, because he had never faced a problem that he couldn't overcome. He found many ways to make a place for himself in peoples' hearts, by voluntarily offering his help, by making spontaneous gifts, and by befriending friendless kids, although if he stayed long enough, the relentless drive to stand out could affect his relationships. His closest friend, Pete Willingham, was his frequent collaborator, but in spelling contests at school, Carlos gladly surpassed Pete, and rubbing it in, tarnished their friendship. In conversations, he steered away from serious subjects, was always cheerful and helpful, and he kept his relationships light, for the most part.

He was cocky and full of bravado, always in motion. He was friends with everyone he met, and everyone liked him. He would never fail to take an opportunity to make a vivid impression on everyone, whether strangers, adults, friends, fellow students, or girls. Although he was short, he was dark, handsome, and quick, and he was also daring. Certain that luck would always see him through, he would do things that no one else would, taking chances that were hair-raising. He always wore a smile or a sardonic smirk. Things always seemed to revolve around Carlos, and he could energize a room. Like his father, he was armed with lots of jokes and stories, and he loved a good time.

Unlike his father, he had few reservations about what constituted a good time. His father respected conventions and was scrupulous about his moral character and behavior.

Carlos wasn't concerned with boundaries, but he idolized his father and practiced his father's behavior in other ways. When he was fourteen, riding his bicycle, he witnessed an altercation between two men that had spilled out of a bar and onto the road and threatened to turn into a gunfight.

Carlos stopped his bike, put it down, and walked over to the larger of the two men. "Excuse me, sir, have you seen my father?" asked Carlos.

"Get lost, kid, I'm a little busy having a conversation here!" said one man.

"I can see that," said Carlos, "which is why my father is on his way."

"What are you talking about, kid?" asked the man.

"My father's the US Marshal here, and I'm pretty sure he'll be interested in your conversation."

Upon which, the two adversaries glared at each other, dusted themselves off, and stalked away in opposite directions.

Carlos was adventurous, and once when he was thirteen and his brother was ten, Carlos approached his younger brother with what he thought was a great idea. "Ed, let's hop one of the freight trains that stop in Ada."

"Where would we go?" asked Ed, Jr.

"Wherever it takes us!" said Carlos. "That's the whole point! It'll be an adventure." They packed sandwiches and water to sustain them on their adventure. Days later, when they were in South Dakota, the train made a stop in the switching yards, and the conductor inspected the freight cars, discovering the two boys.

He took them into the station. Carlos noted a small pin worn by the conductor and recognized it. "Say, Mister, I recognize that pin. My father wears one just like it!"

"Is that a fact, young man?" said the conductor.

It turned out the man was a Freemason, and the boys explained that their father was also a Mason. It is thought that the idea of Masonic brotherhood descends from a sixteenth-century legal definition of a "brother" as one who has taken an oath of mutual support to another. Accordingly, Masons swear at each degree of their advancement in the association to keep the contents of that rank secret, and to support and protect their brethren unless they have broken the law. The conductor telegraphed the rail station in Ada, asking them to tell the boys' mother that he had found them, and then he sent several other telegrams. He arranged to put them on a southbound train, and they were passed on their journey from one Masonic train conductor to another, until they were returned to Ada.

Children received their early schooling in multigrade classes, as was typical in rural communities in those days. Carlos was involved in a wide range of student activities. At age fifteen, he was mentioned several times in the local newspaper, reporting on a football game between Ada Normal (High School) and a local school for the deaf, Sulphur. Carlos received several passes and scored repeatedly as Ada won the game, 39 to 0. This push to stand out was typical of his behavior.

As he entered young adulthood, he became interested in romance and was spotted in nearby communities "courting young ladies," as the local newspaper, which served as a bulletin, reported. His mother and father, aware that their son was nearing manhood, cautioned him about his interactions with young women, encouraging him to always behave honorably and with integrity, and not to fall into the trap of intimate relations before marriage. They reminded him often of his Christian background and of the responsibility he had to avoid temptation, alcohol (which clouded judgment) and gambling (which was a dangerous vice). He cheerfully reassured them that he was aware of these dangers and promised to always avoid them.

As he neared manhood, Carlos suddenly stopped growing. His grandfather, father, and brothers were all short like him, and his comparatively small stature put him at a disadvantage in sports. He had given up the idea of playing football, as his small size was no match for brawnier farm kids who were still growing. Nevertheless, he was determined to turn fate to his advantage, finding other challenges, and overcoming them. In 1916, when he was eighteen and in college at East Central State Normal College, he won the Boy's Reading event at a literary track-and-field meet. He played in the college marching band, often accompanying the football team to statewide games. He was developing characteristics that would mark him throughout his life: competitive, determined, adaptable, outgoing, energetic, adventurous, impulsive. He collected friends like others collected marbles, baseball cards, and Indian-head pennies. It was less about their individual characteristics than about their number, and less about how much he appreciated them than what they could do for him or his ego.

CHAPTER SEVEN

ROMANCE—1916 TO 1917

In those days, the best way to travel from town to town was by rail. A Santa Fe spur line connected Ada to Oklahoma City, where numerous main rail routes were available to Tulsa and points beyond. As a freshman member of East Central's band, Carlos traveled with the football team to cities throughout the state during football season. He still loved football, having played in high school, and rooting for his teams. He enjoyed these trips, which often included stops at the railway depot restaurants, a chain known as "Harvey Houses." These highly successful establishments offered quick, clean, and inexpensive service and good meals for passengers on short layovers. Part of Harvey's business strategy was to hire attractive young women as "servers" (never "waitresses"). The standards were quite high for these young ladies, who were known as "Harvey Girls." They had to have a minimum of an eighth-grade education, good moral character, manners, and be neat and articulate. They also had to agree to a renewable six-month contract during which time they must abide by all company rules and avoid marriage. In return, they got good wages, free room and board, and smart uniforms.

In September, at the start of classes and the football season, the team and the band traveled north by train, and Carlos visited the restaurant in Oklahoma City with some friends from the band. They entered, sat down at a booth, and a young woman gave them menus and cheerfully took their orders. Her manner was vivacious, and the starched white outfit that she wore made her features stand out. While the others were deliberating, Carlos turned to the server and asked, "What's your name, Miss?"

"Why I'm Jo Andrews," she said, smiling widely.

Carlos smiled back at her and said, "I've never met a girl named Joe before, especially not one so pretty!"

That brought a laugh from Jo, and she said, "It's short for Josephine, you dope!"

Carlos guffawed and asked her if she always worked here and what her hours were.

She said, "I work most days, with Mondays off, from eleven to seven," she said.

Carlos said, "You know, I travel a lot with the football team, and we almost always go by train through Oklahoma City. In fact, next Saturday I'll be through here again at about one o'clock, and I'd love to see you then."

"Well, sure, come back then and I'll keep an eye out for you!" Jo replied. "Where are you coming from?" she asked.

"From Ada," he said. "I go to East Central there."

"Oh, really!" she said, "That's my home too. I'm just working here with my sister because it's such a good-paying job and we get free room and board."

"Swell, I bet we know lots of people in common," he said. "It'll be fun to compare notes. I'll see you then, and I won't bring all these other goons with me," said Carlos.

The following weekend, the team traveled through Oklahoma City again, and sure enough, Jo was waiting for him.

"I wasn't sure you were going to show up," said Jo.

"Wouldn't have missed this for the world," said Carlos. "I haven't thought about anything else since last time."

Which was just what Jo was thinking. "That's sweet of you to say," she said.

"I'm just a sweet guy, getting sweet on you. Say, if I can arrange to come back through on Sunday, will you go out with me that night? Since Monday's your day off, I mean."

"Yes, absolutely. I'd really like that," said Jo.

So it was that a romance began between the two youngsters. Over the coming months, Carlos saw Jo as often as he could, arranging his band schedule to the extent possible. Carlos met with Jo for various lengths of time, sometimes with the team, and traveling on his own when that wasn't possible. Jo arranged to meet with him and see him on her hours off duty. The two found that they shared a love of music and the current hits. On Sunday nights they often went together to the movies. It was sensational to see a drama, or a comedy unfold on the screen. They both loved Charlie Chaplin films: The Tramp and The Pawnshop were two of their favorites. They were awed by D. W. Griffith's Birth of a Nation. They enjoyed each other's company and soon fell deeply in love, and they began thinking of a life together.

Carlos was thinking how lucky he was, and certain he would be successful, he thought of leaving school to get a job and earn some money so the two of them could plan their future. He had heard from one of his friends that the Atlantic Oil Company was hiring in Tulsa, and he decided to visit there and apply for a job. Dressed in his best suit, he walked into the office and asked the receptionist, "Who do I have to talk to about applying for a job here, Miss?"

Liking his looks and manner, the young lady said, "Why, my boss, Mr. Robinson. What's your name?" After he told her his name she said, "Just wait here a minute, and I'll see if he's busy."

Carlos inspected the photographs of drilling rigs than hung on the office wall, for a few seconds before the receptionist came back and said, "Okay, he'll see you now."

Carlos entered the office and shook Robinson's hand, saying, "Thanks for seeing me on such short notice, sir."

"Of course, please take a seat, young man. What can I do for you? I understand you're looking for work?"

"Yes, sir. I'll be honest with you, sir. I don't have any experience on drilling rigs or that kind of work, but I like working with people and I'm a quick learner."

"Well, that's not necessarily a bad thing, Carlos. Just about anyone can be a wildcatter and work on a rig, but it so happens what we need right now are personable young men to be scouts, or land men, looking for places where the company can lease drilling sites. I happen to think you just might fill the bill. How soon could you start?"

"Gosh, really? That sounds great! I can start next week, if that's okay," said Carlos.

So, having made the impromptu decision to drop out of college and relocate, Carlos set about arranging his move. When he told Jo that he had some news to share, she said, "Oh, Carlos, I'm excited for you, but we'll still be separated. I was hoping you could find something in Oklahoma City."

"Well, sweetheart, you know what they say about a bird in the hand. I just couldn't turn this down. Besides, I know Harvey House is in Tulsa, too, and maybe you could get transferred there and then we'd be together."

So, Jo, along with her sister Minnie, arranged to get a transfer to the Harvey House in Tulsa, and Carlos and Jo became an ever-closer couple. On her days off, Jo would stay overnight with Carlos at his rooming house, being careful to sneak her in after dusk without the landlady knowing. It's not that Jo's morals were loose. She desperately loved Carlos and was certain that they had a future together.

One October evening, after she joined him in Tulsa, Carlos and Jo crept up the outside back stairs to his garage apartment. Turning back to Jo, Carlos said, "Shhh! Don't wake the old bat up!" Jo giggled with the excitement of it all, and when they were inside, she fell into his arms.

"Oh, Carlos, I've missed you so much, even though it's only been a short time since I last saw you!" she said.

"Honey, it can't be anything like as much as I've missed you. We're going to have a wonderful two days."

"But you know I only get one day off, dear; I can't take an extra day off no matter how much I want to."

"Well, you can take a sick day, can't you? Don't tell me your contract doesn't allow you to get sick?"

And so, the couple had a wonderful time together. They danced to the record player, they sang, and Carlos played "Pretty Baby" on his trumpet until the landlady banged on his door. They went back to the state fair in Oklahoma City together and saw all the wonders, the bright lights, noise, and crowds of people. Carlos was amazed at the livestock exhibits, and they talked about how in the future they might have a big ranch, either in Oklahoma or Texas, or maybe California. Carlos had big dreams, and high hopes as well.

CHAPTER EIGHT

HOMECOMING IN ADA

Finally, at Christmas, Carlos took Jo to Ada to meet his family, and afterward, she took him to meet hers. It had snowed the night before, and they left deep footprints in the gleaming, white blanket. The outside air was crisp and quiet, and all sounds seemed muffled as they walked up the steps, stamping their feet to remove the snow that clung to their shoes. Jo met Marshal Ed, Miss Sue (which is what people outside the family called his mother), sister Maude (sister Belle was married and living in Texas), and brother Max. The couple explained how they had met each other, leaving out the sleepover arrangements. It was obvious that marriage could be in their future, and Max was uneasy. After all, it wouldn't be right if the spotlight fell on Carlos and his marriage before Max, since Max was the oldest boy. Furthermore, Max was home on leave from the army, and his military service and forthcoming posting overseas had interrupted his plans to marry his sweetheart, Billie. Although Max pretended to be pleased for them, inside he was very distressed.

Max smiled and said, "Little brother, I'm so happy for the two of you. You make a fine young couple, and it's obvious you like each other a lot. But you're both so young; you've got all the time in the world to make sure you're right for each other. Carlos, now that you're working, what kind of future do you see for yourself with Atlantic? You'll want to be sure you're on solid ground before you make any big steps," said Max.

"I am being careful," said Carlos. "Things are going great at work, and I've got my own place. Don't worry, Max, I can take care of myself."

"All I'm saying is, before you make any big decisions, just be sure you can take care of yourself and one more," offered Max.

Irritated by Max's effort to belittle their relationship, Carlos replied, "Thanks for your concern, Brother. I'll look to your example," answered Carlos.

Carlos's introduction to Jo's parents went more smoothly. They were more accustomed to her independence and were open-minded about respecting the obvious attraction the young couple had for each other. "Jo, your parents are terrific," said Carlos. "They made me feel so welcome. I'm sorry the reception wasn't better on my side."

"Oh, don't worry about it, dear," said Jo. "What matters is the way we feel about each other, not your brother's opinion."

"He's a bit of a horse's ass, wasn't he?" said Carlos. And they both broke into laughter.

Early the next year, Carlos persuaded Jo to move in with him. She was happy to do so but continued to work at her job, swearing her sister to secrecy. In March, however, she discovered that she was pregnant, and later that year, she returned to Ada to be with her mother for the delivery. Her baby was born in December, a boy. They named him Thomas, after Carlos's father, and Dwight, after a favorite uncle of hers. And of course, they gave him Carlos's last name, no matter that they weren't yet married. Carlos was pleased to accept the congratulations of their friends, but he was genuinely concerned about what the reaction of his parents would be when they learned he had a child out of wedlock. It happened often enough but was nonetheless frowned upon and considered scandalous by many. Carlos was also nervous about being a father. He had no particular interest in children and was not as comfortable around them as he was with adults. His finances were shaky, and he was concerned about the financial responsibilities of caring for a family, especially because he was just twenty years old with an incomplete education, no training, and a meager income.

When the next Christmas came a few weeks later, and the family gathered in Ada again, Carlos asked Jo to celebrate with her own parents rather than with his family. He would use the opportunity to prepare the groundwork for bringing her and the baby into the family, he said. Unfortunately, when Carlos broached the subject with his parents, with Max present, he didn't get the reaction he hoped for. His parents were stunned at the news.

Before their parents could respond, Max spoke up, berating Carlos for being irresponsible. "Carlos, this is so typical of you! You haven't given any thought at all for the honor and reputation of our family name! And you're thoughtless about the disgrace you've brought on our parents." He ranted that Jo was just a gold digger and had loose morals, that their marriage would end in disaster.

Carlos tried to reason with them, irritated that Max had exaggerated and twisted everything he said. "Mother, Father, it's not like Max is saying at all! Jo is a wonderful, sweet girl. She has good morals too. If she was such a gold digger, I doubt she would have picked me. We're in love, that's all there is to it!"

But his mother and father were noncommittal, wanting to discuss the matter privately, rather than in front of their sons. "Let us think this over, Carlos," his mother said, "we need a little time to think about what all this means."

Later that evening, Max slipped out of the house and walked over to the Andrews's home and asked to speak with Jo. When she came, carrying the baby, Max said, "Is that the little bastard? He doesn't look anything like Carlos. Who was actually the father? Some guy you picked up at that pancake house where you worked?"

He kept on disparaging Jo and her attachment to Carlos, berating her for trying to intrude into their family. He only paused when Jo's father came into the vestibule to see what all the noise was about. Soon the two men were shouting at each other, and Jo was in tears, backing away.

The next day, when Carlos came over, she described what had happened and how Max had attacked her so viciously. Carlos was furious and realized that the furor that Max had stirred up was going to at least delay their plans, if not wreck them. He tried to calm Jo down, soothing her, saying nothing had changed, even though he knew it had. They agreed that she should remain with her parents, since his apartment and income were too small to support the three of them, and he would try to find something better.

CHAPTER NINE

THE YANKS ARE COMING—1917-1918

Although war in Europe broke out in 1914, the United States remained on the sidelines until 1917, when Carlos was still nineteen and was courting Jo. America had been firmly in the grip of isolationism, and President Wilson had declared the United States neutral when fighting began in Europe. Regardless of the threats to European countries facing the advancing armies of Germany and the Austro-Hungarian Empire, Americans resisted involvement.

It was only after the interception of a secret diplomatic communication from the German Foreign Office in early 1917, known as the Zimmermann Telegram, which proposed an alliance between Germany and Mexico if the US entered the war against Germany, that the Congress and the administration realized the threat could no longer be ignored. In April of 1917, President Wilson requested a declaration of war against Germany before a joint session of Congress. Wilson cited Germany's violation of its pledge to suspend unrestricted submarine warfare in the North Atlantic as well as its perfidy in soliciting an alliance with Mexico against the United States as his reasons. The Senate and the House voted support soon after.

However, the US Army at that time was merely a small constabulary force of soldiers. Both the country and the army were unprepared for what was going to happen. The United States had no process in place to build a mass army, supply it, or deploy it.

Continental European powers had a universal military service program in place, and when war broke out, their reservists—already trained—went to their mobilization points and joined their units. The United States would work with the Allies, but the troops would remain under US command.

While many American men rushed to recruiting stations and enlisted, the War Department recommended a draft to build what was called the National Army. The Selective Service Act passed on May 18, 1917, and all men aged twenty-one to thirty were required to register with local draft boards. As the war continued, the age for registration went up to forty-five, and the entry level was reduced to age eighteen. Overall, about 24 million men registered for the draft, and inductees comprised 66 percent of those who served.[2]

Wilson established the first modern propaganda office, the Committee on Public Information. Its aim was primarily the American public, and its purpose was to inundate the public with information about how individuals could and should contribute to the war effort, through pamphlets, news releases, magazine ads, campaigns, and films. Patriotic fervor was building, and the president and his military leaders needed to rapidly expand America's armed forces. Soon signs everywhere said: "Uncle Sam Wants You!" Mothers were encouraged to send their sons to serve. It got so that people would glare at physically able young men who should be in the trenches, defending their nation. Just before he turned twenty, Carlos went back to Ada, and he and Jo decided to wait to get married. Considering the best way to improve his opportunities, he re-enrolled in East Central College, where his younger brother, Ed, was in his freshman year. Swept up by enthusiasm, both were eager to show their patriotism by signing up for the Draft Board Registration together in September of 1918. Ed falsified his age to qualify. Their older brother, Max, had registered two years before and was already in the army.

___

[2] *World War I: Building the American Military*, Jim Garamone, US Department of Defense, March 29, 2017

Hat in hand, he went to see Jo, and explained that he had to do his duty and join the army. He was beaming, certain that Jo would be proud of him for his patriotism. As soon as he could, he would come back for her, and once he had a good job—maybe get on as a ranch hand in California—they would be married.

This plan caught Jo completely by surprise. By going into the army, she felt he was deserting her. "I don't believe you!" Jo said. "There's no reason, other than your brother Max, that we can't marry right now! Why did you sign up for the army? I think you were just looking for an excuse to avoid marrying me and taking care of our son." Jo was heartbroken and dissolved in tears. Carlos was embarrassed because he knew she was right. He tried to reassure and comfort her, but she pushed him away. "You don't care anything about me! You don't care anything about our baby! Just leave us alone because that's all you want!"

She regretted these words as soon as she said them, but she was too upset to take them back. Humiliated, she returned to Tulsa with their son, staying in a hotel and working as a cashier, hoping that Carlos would follow her. When he didn't come for her, her parents came to her rescue and took Jo and the baby to return to the family home in Pennsylvania. Later, Jo regretted her harsh words and wrote to Carlos. He replied that he still loved her and would try to make things work out. Nonetheless, he was relieved to have escaped these responsibilities.

Soon after registering, Carlos and Ed joined the Student Army Training Corps and were enlisted. The SATC was the forerunner of the ROTC and was administered by the War Department in Washington for the purpose of training officer candidates and technical experts. Carlos was in the officer section, and Ed was in a vocational section. The training programs were conducted at about six hundred colleges, universities, professional, technical and trade schools. Members were inducted and became members of the army on active duty, receiving pay and subsistence, subject to military orders, and living in barracks under military discipline in exactly the same manner as any other soldier.[3]

---

[3] *The Student Army Training Corps*, Second Edition, Descriptive Circular, October 14, 1918

One weekend, eager to impress everyone, and especially their father, Carlos and Ed came home in their uniforms: Carlos in officer's garb of boots and garrison cap, Ed in a private's puttees and campaign hat. They posed proudly for a photograph with their father. While they looked at the camera, proud of their valor, the Marshal looked into the distance, thinking of the peril they might face, having experienced so much danger himself.

The war ended two months after they registered, on November 11, 1918, and as luck would have it, unlike their brother Max, the younger brothers were never deployed to war. There was a short period of time while they remained enlisted, until they were eventually mustered out. Carlos was relieved to have avoided danger.

CHAPTER TEN

THE SPANISH FLU

At the very same time, the nation was afflicted with the Spanish Influenza, or Spanish Flu. The misnamed Spanish Flu, which wasn't Spanish and was much more virulent than common influenza, had been raging in Europe and made its first appearance in America on March 4, 1918, when an army private at Fort Riley, Kansas, came down with symptoms. As more soldiers returned home from Europe, the disease became much more widespread with a second wave in the fall. News of the pandemic had been drowned out by news of the war gripping Europe, and America's involvement. The virus, which we now know as H1N1, began appearing in Oklahoma in September 1918. There soon were official denials and public confusion. Officials minimized the health dangers, rapidly rising infections and deaths. Misinformation was widespread, and the economy was affected. With medicine in short supply, and no known cure, physicians were prescribing dram bottles of whiskey to be filled at police stations from confiscated supplies. When word got out that whiskey helped flu sufferers feel better, moonshiners and bootleggers did a brisk trade with the price of a quart reaching the equivalent of $234 in today's dollars. Ultimately, more Americans were killed by the Spanish Flu than in the war. Once again, fate had intervened to save Carlos. From that point, events unfolded rapidly.

CHAPTER ELEVEN

1919 TO THE EARLY 1920S—CALIFORNIA OR BUST

Although Jo didn't know it, she wasn't the only girl who Carlos had connected with on his travels. During one of the college football games in Durant, he ran across an acquaintance from his class in Ada. Just as Carlos was exiting the stadium with the band, a group of young women who had been watching the game joined them on the ramp. One of them looked familiar. "Bess Davis, is that you?" Carlos yelled. "Wait a second and let me catch up!"

Bess was a pretty girl, and they had first met in English class. He really liked her personality; she was wickedly funny. "I didn't expect to see you here. It's great that you came down to see the Tigers play!"

"I'm from Durant, silly, don't you remember? Gosh, Carlos, I didn't realize you're in the band. They were terrific at halftime."

"Thanks, and yeah, I did forget you're from Durant. Well, even though you're from here, you must have been cheering for East Central, right?" he said, chuckling.

Her eyebrows lifted as she replied, "I was rooting for both teams. My brother plays for Southeastern, so I guess although I go to East Central, I was also rooting for the Savages."

"So then, you win either way! That's okay, I forgive you," said Carlos with a grin. "I've got a brother who plays for the Tigers, so I understand. Say, I've got a couple hours before we catch the train back to Ada. Do you want to go somewhere and get a soda or something?"

"Sure, why not? Let me just tell the other girls where I'm going."

It all began innocently enough, but soon Carlos was juggling his feelings and his time between two women. It was kind of risky, but kind of fun too. Besides, he wasn't as serious about Bess, not like Jo, and it was not like he was married or anything. She was just a friend. But the two continued to see each other from time to time outside of class and drew closer. He was fascinated by her mischievousness. After Jo left for the East with their baby, Carlos mustered out of the army and began seeing a lot more of Bess. At first, it was just soda dates, where they would meet at the drug store soda fountain. Then, he asked her out to the motion pictures. Like Jo, Bess shared his enjoyment of movies. Then they went out on picnics, and soon they were necking in the back of his car. They began talking about marriage when Bess discovered she was pregnant. This time, he accepted his fate. On a visit back to Ada to see his family, he went to Durant, saw Bess, and proposed to her. She readily agreed, and their plan was for them to relocate to California so they could avoid scandalous rumors. He left East Central to go out to California to arrange things and seek his fortune. He heard there were lots of great jobs out there, and he was sure that he could get ahead fast. Soon, there appeared in the Ada Evening News, an announcement of an important new event in his life:

August 18, 1919:
The proud parents announce the marriage of their son Carlos Benson, to Miss Bess Davis, of Durant, Oklahoma, at 10:30 Saturday morning, August 16th, at the home of the groom's sister, Mrs. J. S. Darnell (Belle), 1255 North Grand, Los Angeles, California.
The bride and groom left immediately after the ceremony for their home at El Centro, California where the groom works at a creamery company.
This is the culmination of a romance of many moons, for it was when Durant and Ada played their first football game and Carlos played in the band that accompanied the ball players to Durant that

Dan Cupid began to weave the net, which now entangles two souls in nuptial bliss.

Carlos had gone to California to stay with his brother, Max, who was living with his wife, Billie, in El Centro, in the Imperial Valley, a broiling hot and dusty agricultural area about 180 miles southeast of Los Angeles. His move was a forerunner of what would later become a great migration of "Okies," some 440,000 of them, who left Oklahoma for California in the 1930s to escape the effects of the Dust Bowl—the meteorological period in which tons of topsoil were stripped from the farms of the southern Midwest and blown eastward, devastating all agriculture in the multistate region. They were married twenty months after the birth of his son to Jo. Jo's mother, in Ada, sent the news clipping to Jo, who was in Tulsa. Jo was shocked and humiliated by the news, but in retrospect, she concluded that although Carlos had been almost ready for marriage, he couldn't marry Jo because of the trouble Max had stirred up.

In November, the *Ada Evening News* published this letter from Carlos:

El Centro, California, November 20, 1919 Dearest East Central: As you march out onto the field to fight for our grand school and you get on your toes for the "game of the season," just remember that "we"—the Durant girl (my wife)—and myself are for you and that we want to see you come through on top!

My wife objects to my saying "we" because we both have brothers playing football on the opposing teams. But nevertheless, when the Evening News comes out with the story of the game, just bundle one up and send it to me.

I must have a yearbook to commemorate our win—so tell the book agents. Gobs o' regards to my old home school! Go for Durant's goat. CARLOS

Less than a year later, in 1920, Carlos was still stocking and sacking groceries in El Centro when Bess gave birth to their daughter,

Barbara Bess. It was the year Prohibition began, making the manufacture, transport, and sale of intoxicating liquor illegal. This really didn't affect Carlos's work, but he had to get more income. With a population of just under six thousand, El Centro didn't offer many opportunities. Soon, Bess and Carlos moved to Long Beach, California, where he had found a job at another grocery that paid much more than he made before. Later, in 1923, Carlos became a Ford car salesman in Los Angeles. He brought Bess and their infant daughter back to Ada for a visit, driving a new Ford. By 1924, the three of them lived in a suburb of LA, and Carlos worked as a building materials dealer.

Their life in California had not turned out to be the stuff of dreams, and money problems made things more difficult for them both. Their temperaments were different too. Bess loved to dance. She wanted Carlos to learn the Charleston, but he didn't enjoy dancing. Anytime the band started up with that energetic music, she would stand up, hold out her hand, and say, "Come on, Carlos, let's go!" He had said he would try it, but he would renege, not willing to go out on the dance floor and embarrass himself. Finally, after many such refusals, Bess would find another male friend, or even a stranger, and whirl on the dance floor with him, while Carlos fumed from the sidelines. As if to underline their differences, they found they couldn't agree on politics. Bess was a Democrat, and Carlos a Republican. He was more conventional in his outlook; she was more open-minded. She said things that got his goat; he said things that got under her skin. In 1921, soon after they were married, they found they had a serious disagreement about the race riot in Tulsa. Carlos believed the stories he read in the papers that the Negroes were rioting, and they had caused the destruction that followed. Bess took the opposite view, citing reports that white hooligans started the riot and were responsible for causing the fires and damage. Their disagreements continued to simmer. During the presidential election of 1924, he was all for "that nincompoop, Calvin Coolidge" as Bess called him. She was torn between John Davis because he shared her maiden name, and what Carlos referred to as "that radical Socialist" Bob La Follette, because Davis was nearly as reactionary as Coolidge. When Coolidge won decisively, Carlos rubbed it in, while she fumed in resentment.

Bess started figuratively hitting Carlos below the belt. "When are you going to quit jumping from job to job?" she asked him. "Why can't you find something that pays enough for us to live on?"

"Oh yeah?" Carlos hit back, "Why don't you get off your fat ass and help out?"

"I don't see you taking care of the baby, helping around the house, doing errands, or paying the bills!" she responded. "Face it, you're all hat and no cattle; you don't have any real skills that anybody wants. You're a big fat failure!"

He stormed out of the house, slamming the door behind him. *Good riddance!* she thought.

The next year, in 1925, Carlos and Bess at last decided that California wasn't working out, and they moved back to Tulsa, Oklahoma, hoping that a return to familiar territory would relieve their stress. Carlos joined with his brothers to form "Three Brothers Real Estate," but as all three were novices in the field, with no contacts or networks, their prospects were dismal to nonexistent. That same year, Carlos and Bess separated. Bess had had enough, and this was the last straw. She was realistic enough to see that things were not likely to change soon, and her future with Carlos was bleak.

And so, Bess brought up the subject of a divorce. "Carlos, I'm not happy, and I can see clearly that you aren't either. We're not doing ourselves any favors by continuing like this."

Carlos, however, wasn't prepared to admit to himself, his parents, or to his brother Max that his marriage was a failure. "But what about the effect on little Barbara? Shouldn't we try to patch things up for her sake?"

"Carlos, you know that won't work. She's five years old, and in all that time, things have only gotten worse between us. Plus, it's clear you really aren't concerned about Barbara; you never pay any attention to her at all. And I really don't want to go on this way."

Seeing that her mind was made up, Carlos gave in. "Okay, just be sure you tell her that this was your idea, not mine."

"I'm not telling her anything until she's older," Bess said. She soon filed for divorce, and after it was granted, quickly vanished, taking their daughter Barbara with her. Carlos would never see or hear from either of them again. Barbara would ultimately meet her future husband at the University of Mississippi and become a successful interior decorator in Kentucky, leaving behind two sons and a daughter. None of them would ever be in contact with Carlos or his family again. Carlos considered the end of their relationship good news.

CHAPTER TWELVE

1925 TO 1926—AN ADVENTURE IN TEXAS

After Carlos's misadventures in California and Tulsa, where his first marriage began falling apart and his prospects dwindled, he returned home to Ada and searched for something more permanent. He desperately needed some steady work. His father, a US Marshal in the Prohibition era, was still roaming the countryside, tracking down bootleggers and raiding stills, amassing huge piles of bottled firewater that had found its way into Indian encampments as far away as Minnesota and the Dakotas. His workload had exploded, with Prohibition in full force and a segment of the population determined to thwart it. Although Marshal Ed's territory included Texas, he was so busy that he rarely ventured back down to the state where he had spent his youth. Carlos had heard about wild parties in college fraternity houses in Texas that were fueled by booze, which was apparently plentiful despite the Prohibition. With his father, whom he had accompanied on several raids while he was younger, Carlos worked out an arrangement where he would go to Texas and serve (unofficially) as a federal prohibition officer to investigate the sources of this illegal alcohol. He would be paid subsistence and expenses while on assignment. They decided that the best place to start would be in Austin, at the University of Texas.

Carlos's education had stopped before he had completed his courses at East Central Normal, and he wasn't qualified to enter the university, especially as an out-of-state student. The registrar balked at admitting him because that quota was filled and he couldn't afford the tuition. However, Carlos remembered that his uncle in Sherman, Texas, bank president William Rufus, had served on the Board of Regents at the University from 1917 to 1921, and once offered to help Carlos get admitted there. Uncle William continued as a university benefactor, with influential friends still on the board. Urged on by Carlos, Marshal Ed contacted his brother and arranged his assistance in persuading the administration to make an exception for Carlos. They reluctantly permitted him to enter, posing as a freshman, in September 1925.

At first, Carlos was overwhelmed when he saw the huge campus, built on forty acres of donated land and with an enrollment of more than four thousand students, compared to East Central with less than two hundred students. His assignment was to audit courses, giving the appearance of being an out-of-state student, while befriending other students to identify the sources of bootlegged alcohol. He managed, again with his uncle's help, to secure a room in B Hall, the only on-campus men's dormitory, thinking it was the best way to quickly make friends. His roommate, Frederick Johnson, or "Fred," was from Waco, and was also a freshman, whose father had exercised his benefactor status to get his son into the highly popular dorm. It was inexpensive, centrally located, and offered opportunities to quickly access any point on the campus.

Carlos, who was nearly twenty-eight, was older than most freshman students, but because of his small size didn't look it. Nevertheless, he was comparatively self-assured and knew how to be likeable. Carlos's roommate Fred, unlike Carlos, was tall and thin, with sandy-colored hair, fair skin, and still afflicted with teenage acne. Fred was reserved in manner. The pair looked and behaved like polar opposites. Carlos took Fred under his wing and introduced him to others as he met them. The two spent weekends together on campus, and Fred turned out to have a knack for poker matching that of Carlos. Despite, or because of his reticent nature, he was a natural-born bluffer. The two started playing poker, joining groups of freshmen and upperclassmen, and alcohol was often available, accompanied by ragtime and jazz on the radio. The city's progressive radio station, KNOW, played Louis Armstrong's Chicago and New Orleans style of jazz. Anything but that damned Charleston. This was music to listen to, not to just jump around to like a halfwit. Carlos began cultivating ties with the young men who bought the moonshine, while also making friends in his classes. Within a short time, Carlos had a widening circle of friends. He concentrated on those who were the most boisterous, and those who were most likely to break rules and take risks. To gain their trust, Carlos played along, and with his dark, swarthy good looks, he became known as "the life of the party." He grew a mustache to reinforce the mystery of his background and further set himself apart from the other college kids. Carlos gave his garrulous personality free reign. He became well known for his wisecracks, matched by his sardonic humor. While Fred was winning at the table, Carlos made side bets, backing his roommate. He would also make audacious bluffs, himself. Once, he faced down four other players who folded against his pair of twos. But he wouldn't show his cards. "Why should I? You guys wouldn't pay to see 'em," meanwhile showing his hand to Fred, who nodded, deadpan. As a result, you never knew if he was making an outrageous bluff, or if he really had the cards.

He also became known for his capacity for alcohol, often outdrinking everyone at parties and at the poker table. "Hey, Don Carlos, save some for us!" said some of his friends, to laughter all around. He had picked up the nickname at one party when he showed up wearing a sombrero. He nurtured the moniker, and with his swarthy complexion, it stuck with him.

"I will, as soon as you bring some to the party!" said Carlos, with a wide grin. Carlos had a way of finding whiskey when it was tough to locate.

He was making headway, discovering the sources of the spirits. He identified the students who seemed to supply the campus and carefully nourished friendships among them, which required a greater level of trust than his easier friendships among the partygoers. One of these suppliers was Gordy Neuman, a senior from

Seguin. Gordy's uncle ran a still just outside of San Antonio, and through his network was introduced to some bootleggers who ran stills near Austin. Through that connection, Gordy maintained an impressive income by selling booze to trusted fellow students.

One afternoon, Carlos approached Gordy and asked to buy a jug of whiskey. "Say, Gordy, I'm having a poker party on Friday night, and I'd like to serve some liquid refreshment. I've heard that you might know where I could find some. And if you would like to come, and I'd be happy to pay you for it."

Gordy said, "I don't know where you heard that, Carlos. Someone must have given you some bad info, but I'd be happy to come, and I can ask around for you. Where's it going to be?"

"That's swell," said Carlos. "I booked a room at the Driscoll Hotel, and we'll each pitch in five bucks to pay the tab. If you can find some hootch, you can get in free. Check-in time is six o'clock."

"Okay, fine. I'll ask some of my friends if they know anyone and let you know. How many guys are coming?"

"It's a small group. We'll be nine guys at two tables, and we'll rotate around so everyone can meet everybody else."

"Swell," said Gordy. "I'll be in touch."

Gordy had friends who were acquainted with Carlos, and immediately, he looked one up. "Hey, Sam," he said, "how well do you know that guy Don Carlos? Is he Mexican? What do you know about him?"

Sam Murphy replied, "Yeah, I know him. He's a veteran from Oklahoma who got wounded and sidetracked by the war, and so now he's catching up. He seems like a good guy, likes to party, he's a smart cookie and kind of a wise ass. Why, what's up?"

"He asked me if I know where he can get some 'shine for a party he's throwing Friday. I got a little suspicious, is all. You know the sheriff sometimes plants a rat in the student body to sniff out suppliers. I just want to be careful. What's with the moniker, anyway—Don Carlos?"

"I don't know, it's just what everybody calls him. He's not a Mex; I think it's just a nickname. I don't blame you for being careful. Tell you what, I'll check around and see what else I can find out about him."

"That'd be great. It's one thing if the guy's legit, but if he's not, he might have a little accident and his party might have to get cancelled," said Gordy with a wink and a smile.

"I catch your drift," said Sam with a serous expression. "I'll get back to you."

The next day, Sam came by Gordy's apartment. "Well, I found out a little bit more. As the guy tells it, he was some kind of war hero, got wounded in France, and by the time he got out of the hospital, the armistice was signed. He rooms with another freshman named Fred Johnson, who's a kind of quiet guy from Waco. Says Carlos talks about getting a degree in business and wants to run a company. Because he's from Oklahoma, it's not likely he's got any connection to the sheriff here."

"Okay, thanks, Sam. Maybe I'll find someone who can find him some juice then. I appreciate the intel."

By January 1926, after making many purchases of "evidence" himself, Carlos in this way slowly had identified and located several operating distilleries in the hot, scrubby hills west of Austin. Carlos knew that once these stills were raided, his cover could be blown, and his masquerade finished. He contacted his father, who put him in touch with local law enforcement officers and they hatched a plan. They would simultaneously sweep the largest bootleggers to frighten the area's illegal industry and disrupt their operations.

Keeping their meetings as quiet as possible, Carlos and agents from the Travis County sheriff's department gathered on the west side of Austin to plan their moves. Late one Thursday evening in February of 1926, Carlos and members of the department grouped near several locations in the hills west of Austin and raided four operators. Several bootleggers were arrested.

The lawmen's operation was like some that Carlos had experienced while accompanying his father as a teenager in Oklahoma. On one of those raids, a bootlegger had rigged a "wolf gun" device, with a string attached to the trigger and deployed in the main approach to the still. As the Marshal and his posse approached, a dog accompanying them tripped the string and was killed by the shotgun blast. Remembering his experience, Carlos warned the other agents to avoid the most obvious paths to the stills in case a similar defense had been set up by these bootleggers.

The raids gained national attention and galvanized the remaining bootleggers, who warned of violence if the raids continued. Reporters from several newspapers eventually contacted Carlos, who had been open about orchestrating the raids. He briefed them on the raids and results and wove into his narrative his experiences with the wolf gun, hinting that he and his party had been fired upon, but his good luck had saved him. He told reporters that the team of lawmen expected more than thirty arrests and the confiscation of over a hundred gallons of whiskey. The story gained fleeting national attention, and Carlos enjoyed the notoriety. However, now that his cover story was blown, he was in danger from Gordy and the bootleggers, and so, for his safety, Carlos had to promptly leave Austin and the university behind. He would not follow in his father's footsteps. He liked making friends, partying, and all the attention, but did not like the danger.

CHAPTER THIRTEEN

1927 TO 1936—NEW ROMANCES

C arlos's brother Ed had landed a job with Texaco (the Texas Oil Company) in Houston, and after routing the bootleggers, Carlos joined Ed there to look for work. That summer, their father suffered a stroke, and both sons returned to Ada to be with their parents. Returning to Houston afterward, Carlos spent the days pounding the sidewalks, looking for a job. During this time, when the two brothers were rooming together, Ed came across a letter written to Carlos from a woman named Jo. It was a love letter, and it contained a sentimental poem filled with longing and nostalgia. Ed could recite this poem years later, word for word, and he often wondered who Jo was, and why she had written to his brother.

"Carlos, did you have a serious relationship with anyone before Bess?" Ed asked his brother.

"Naw, nothing much. I played the field, as they say," Carlos said, rebuffing Ed's probes about his personal life. Carlos clearly didn't want to discuss it, and Ed just filed it away in his mental folder labeled "Carlos's Secrets."

Carlos still had no other prospects, but one day, fate sent him a gift. Although Carlos, having put on some pounds over the years, was a rather a slob in private, he was always a fastidious dresser when in public, and he frequented a "valet shop" on Grant Street in what is now the Montrose area in Houston. This was a combination laundry, dry cleaning, and alterations shop that was owned by a young woman named Opal. Whenever Carlos dropped by, the two of them bantered back and forth, and they enjoyed swapping jokes and gossip. Eventually they began dating, and they grew fond of each other, enjoying each other's company. One of their favorite pastimes was joining Carlos's brother Ed and his girlfriend, Esther, for an outing at Lake Houston or in Galveston. Being near water was a good way to cool off in Houston's sultry summer weather. During the day, it was suffocating and sapped a person's energy. It wasn't until the late afternoon when breezes would build up from the southeast that life became bearable, and even then, the brick houses that most folks lived in radiated heat for hours, like ovens. After months of seeing each other, enjoying heavy "petting sessions," they thought about getting married, but Carlos dragged his feet because his previous experiences had not worked out. Eventually, he gave in. It was clear that Ed and Esther were headed toward marriage, and most of their friends were either married or on their way.

Opal had been married before, when she was only eighteen, and divorced soon afterward. Now she was twenty-nine, about three years older than Carlos. In November, Carlos took Opal to Ada to meet his parents. When they returned, he found some temporary sales work, and they married in a small, civil ceremony.

Carlos always inflated the importance of his work, and Opal believed him for a time, but eventually she began to wonder. She wondered whether she had made a mistake in judgment, marrying this guy who was so convincing but who never showed any results. She was a results-oriented woman, determined to stand on her own two feet and always be in a position to take care of herself and her mother. She had thought that Carlos was a bright, up-and-coming young business leader, or at least had that potential. Now, she wasn't too sure anymore.

It turned out that Opal was the entrepreneur of the two; in addition to the valet shop, she also had investments in real estate, mostly centered in Galveston, nearby on the Gulf Coast. The two newlyweds would take the Interurban train down to the island to inspect properties, collect rent, and scout for new investments. Carlos spun big stories about his real estate conquests a few years ago in Tulsa, and the two of them began thinking about next steps. Within a short period of time, they began having disagreements about investment opportunities, with Carlos urging Opal to make a bigger splash by investing in commercial properties and Opal resisting. Carlos, confident of his success, suggested that she go to her bank to ask for a loan to float one of his "deals." Opal replied, "Why don't you go to your own banker and get the money?"

Carlos didn't have any banking relationships like Opal did and they both knew it, so that seemed to him like a stupid suggestion and a put down. Eventually, however, he thought of his Uncle William, who had helped him get admitted to Texas University. He owned one of the biggest banks in North Texas, and surely, he would be willing to help Carlos out of this bind (a bind that Carlos had created for himself). He carefully constructed his request letter, reminding his uncle of his spectacular success with the raid, describing the huge opportunities with beachfront commercial property in Galveston, and asking if his uncle might recommend a bank that might be interested in financing such deals. He posted the letter and waited, day after day, for a very long time for a reply. He thought how great it would be: You didn't think I had any connections, huh? You thought I was all just hot air, huh? Well, what do you think now?

Finally, just as he decided he needed to telephone his uncle to inquire if he had received the letter, his uncle's reply arrived. Uncle William thanked Carlos for his letter, praised his success in organizing the bootlegger raids, and turned down his request. Carlos couldn't believe it! He was furious, of course, at his uncle's lack of imagination as well as his lack of familial concern. It just proved what everyone in the family said about him: The guy was a heartless moneybag and had abandoned his own people. He decided not to tell Opal about this embarrassing development, hoping he could think of something else.

Opal said that once Carlos invested real money in these deals, he could participate in making decisions, but not before; after all, it was her money. Carlos replied, "You sure know how to cut a guy's nuts off!" to which Opal replied, "How would you know; you haven't got any!" It seemed to Opal that the only thing Carlos had brought to their partnership was an opinion but no real expertise and certainly no cash at all. For Carlos's part, he was bitter that Opal didn't respect his opinions, his abilities, or his background in real estate, law enforcement, or the military. He felt he had wasted his time; she just wasn't yielding or generous—she was too skeptical, independent, cautious, and selfish. He knew what she thought of him, and it was painful because so much of it was true. It seemed like this marriage was headed for the rocks, the same direction as his last one, and soon they divorced.

Meanwhile, Carlos's brother Ed had gotten a position with Chevrolet Motors, a division of General Motors. Headquartered in Detroit, the company was rapidly expanding in the South and southeast, and they were hiring in Houston. During this time, automobiles had captured the imagination of the entire country. An infrastructure was gradually being built up including hard-surfaced roadways and filling stations. Soon, they would be widespread enough that you could travel from coast to coast with no problems other than maybe a flat tire. The styling wasn't too imaginative yet. These cars, built by Fisher Body coachbuilders of Detroit, looked more or less like coaches without horses, but improvements were coming, like suspensions to absorb jostling, padded seats, and roll-up windows.

By summertime, more positions were opening, and Carlos applied and got an interview. The interview went well, and he was made an offer that he quickly accepted. He began a period of training, poring over sales manuals and attending lectures. He was encouraged enough to think about marriage again. Soon enough, he met a young woman, Celine, who worked as a secretary with Ed's girlfriend, Esther. They first dated, got more serious, and then on impulse, Carlos asked her to marry him and she accepted.

Carlos liked his new work; it appealed to him on several levels. He liked the idea of being associated with this modern, technological marvel, the automobile. It was exciting, and as an insider, he would see in advance the design of models the company planned to introduce. He learned that the company planned to build the public excitement by introducing new models every year, with new styling and mechanical improvements. It was like being part of a secret society that had big plans and the power to change the world for the better. He liked almost everyone he worked with; they were smart, fast thinkers, agile, and hard working. He respected the company—it was huge—and he liked the pay. Finally, he was on a decent salary, and there were annual bonuses as well. With the change in Carlos's circumstances, his relationship with Celine improved, along with his self-esteem. His brother Ed was doing well, too, and was thinking about getting married soon to his girlfriend, Esther. Carlos considered himself fortunate that he was finally on a path to success.

In the warm summer weekends, they would all escape the sweltering city. "Let's drive down to the beach at Galveston, Carlos," said Ed. "I'll bring Esther, and you and Celine come too." It was a bit presumptuous since Ed didn't own a car, but he knew that Celine had bought a used Reo convertible a few months ago.

However, Celine was all for the idea. She liked Ed and Esther. "They make a cute couple," she said.

The next Saturday, they drove over and picked up Ed and Esther, and with Carlos behind the wheel and the top down, drove to Galveston. They crossed the causeway and drove to the seawall, and then onto the beach. Carlos thought, Well, it sure isn't California! but he kept that thought to himself as the four of them waded out into the few inches of barely cool, softly rolling, grayish-brown waves. They enjoyed soaking in the brine, splashing each other, yelling and horsing around, the girls shrieking when getting their faces splashed.

Later, they retreated to the beach, lay in the sun, posed for goofy photographs with Ed's camera, and enjoyed the salty Gulf air. After one more dip, they went to the beachside cabanas, changed into dry clothes, and realized how hungry they were. "I'm starved," said Carlos. "What say we go to Gaido's?" That was a favorite seafood restaurant for locals and visitors alike.

"Great idea!" said Ed. They piled into the car and made the short drive back on Seawall Boulevard.

"It's hard to imagine that this town nearly blew completely away during the hurricane," said Celine, referring to the devastating hurricane of 1900.

"Yeah, there's no sign of it now except this seawall," said Carlos. "Hard to believe that they raised the whole island and rebuilt everything. It must have been a huge job!"

They passed a sign on one bait shop that said: FRESH DEAD SHRIMP. "Oh, look at that," said Ed. "How fresh do you think they are? I hope the ones at Gaido's are a little fresher!"

Celine never said much about her past, and that suited Carlos, because he didn't want to talk about his own. She was close to her parents and respected that Carlos was close to his parents. Soon, Carlos was sent to nearby Beaumont, Texas, in 1928, where he did well, and the following year he and Celine were relocated to San Angelo, Texas, where he was promoted to be the district representative for Chevrolet. In November of 1929, Carlos's father, Thomas Edward, the Deputy US Marshal, died of a stroke in Oklahoma, at age sixty-two. Carlos was dismayed to learn of his father's death. He had always seemed to be a larger-than-life figure, a steady and permanent presence in Carlos's life. His absence opened a huge void. Carlos and Celine joined his brothers and sisters in a brief, sad reunion in Ada to bury their father and comfort their mother.

As news of the marshal's death spread, an avalanche of letters began arriving from those who had known him or worked with him, or simply admired him. Stricken by grief, the mail overwhelmed his widow, and she wrote a plea on the back of one of them to her oldest son, Max: "I have some letters that need to be answered. I simply can't, for I can't think straight. I am far from well. Looks like I am going to have to have a complete rest. Took cold and it has settled in my hip, back, and legs; in fact, don't have much to live for any way—so old." She was just fifty-eight but considered "old" by the day's standards. Soon after the burial, Carlos and Celine returned to their home in San Angelo, and Ed and Esther left Max to comfort their mother, as his work was less demanding.

San Angelo was nearly in the geographical center of Texas. As an early frontier town, it was characterized by saloons, prostitution, and gambling. When the town applied for a post office, it became the county seat. The town was surrounded by farms on the east and ranches on the west. It became a feed and watering center for cattle drives on their way to market during the cattle boom of the 1870s. In 1888 and 1909, railroads were completed, and the town became a shipping center for agricultural products. Between 1920 and 1930, the population more than doubled from 10,050 to 25,308, attributable in part to the opening of the Permian Basin oilfield in 1923. It was a prime location for automobile sales. A photograph of West Harris Avenue in the 1930s shows a busy roadway with rows of cars parked on both sides and traffic lights every few blocks. Carlos managed sales and distribution for a growing number of dealerships and service centers in the district.

In March of 1932, Celine gave birth to Carlos's second daughter and third child, Nancy Sue, although Celine knew nothing of the prior offspring. In 1933, the family relocated to Carrizo Springs, Texas, a small town southwest of San Antonio near the border with Mexico. It was a big change from San Angelo and an even bigger change for Celine from Houston. The moves were tough, but the couple made the best of it all, grateful that Carlos was employed during the terrible Great Depression. The timing was fortunate, too, because the Dust Bowl, which was centered at the Oklahoma Panhandle, would wreak havoc on the area surrounding it, culminating on Black Sunday, in April of 1935. Had they remained in San Angelo, car sales would have been affected, and Carlos might have been in big trouble. Prohibition had just ended, and they led an active social life, hosting open houses, bridge parties, and salons, and welcoming Celine's parents on visits from Houston.

In the spring of 1934, the family moved again, from Carrizo Springs to Corpus Christi. The frequent moves were exhausting for Celine. This was the fourth move in just seven years. While Carlos was enjoying his luck and his rapid rise in the company, Celine became tired of the moves, of making new friends and parting from them, of the instability of it all, getting settled, packing up, and moving again, going through the whole process of rebuilding a social life in unfamiliar places over and over. She had done her part, hosting open houses at Christmastime, entertaining all of Carlos's business friends and their wives at parties in their home. She worried about the effect such a life would have on their daughter, Nancy. While Nancy was just a toddler still, soon enough she would need a stable home, school, friends, and a neighborhood. Carlos's mother sent her clothes and shoes, but Celine was too busy to acknowledge the gifts. Furthermore, Celine wanted more for herself. She was dreading the next move, which seemed an integral part of Carlos's work.

But every time she tried to discuss this with Carlos, he was defensive. "Carlos," she said, "I'm so tired of moving. Isn't there any way to settle down in one place for a longer time?'

"Celine, honey, you'll get used to it," he said. "You've been great, and we're a terrific team. It's all part of getting ahead. Plus, I have to go where they need me. It's the only way to grow my career, by taking on new responsibilities."

"I know that," said Celine. "But they can't expect you to keep moving every two years! Think about Nancy. She'll need a home, school, friends. That's going to be impossible if we're always moving."

"Look, don't you think I know that? This moving around has been tough on me too. New situations, new people, more responsibility, more work. It's not like you and Nancy have the hardest job here!"

This really upset Celine and made her angry. "You always just brush me off when I talk about this, as though it's not important—as though I'm not important," she said. "You don't care about me or our marriage or our child!" She grew cross and tired of Carlos, and tired of their marriage that he seemed to take for granted. "You're so consumed with your career that you're willing to make any sacrifice for it, including your family life, not to mention us, your family members."

"Dammit, that's not fair, Celine!" he said. "You say you're tired of me. Well, I'm tired of your carping, finding fault, and mooning around homesick all the time!"

They fought with each other more frequently, each finding spiteful things to say to each other. He couldn't tolerate her lack of support; after all, he was knocking himself out to build a future for their family. It was an investment. He began drinking and saying rude things about her to her friends, arguing, and calling her horrible names.

Once, he came home to find her playing bridge with friends. "Goddammit!" he yelled at Celine. "Why aren't you cooking dinner, you lazy slut?" Turning to the other women, he said "Well, why are you bitches just sitting there? Enjoying the show? Get out, NOW!!" He was beside himself with anger and started throwing objects at the stunned women. They scrambled for their things, then raced each other to the door, slamming it behind them just as a flying glass ashtray broke against the door jamb. Carlos immediately walked over to the bar he had set up in the living room and poured himself two stiff drinks, which he downed one after the other.

By September, they had separated, but they decided to make one last attempt to reconcile by hosting a Christmas open house together, as they had done so many years previously. But this time, Carlos had spiked the punchbowl, and he and Celine both dipped into it a few too many times.

"Celine, honey, can you turn the music down a notch?" Carlos asked. She had turned up the radio when they started playing one of her favorite songs.

"Turn it down yourself, Mr. Big Shot!" said Celine, with a giggle, spilling some of her drink. "Oh, Jesus! Now look what you made me do!" she said.

"I think you've had enough punch, Celine."

"Oh yeah? Well just try and stop me," she said. When Carlos grabbed her wrist, she threw the rest of her drink in his face.

"Goddammit, will you just calm down?" he yelled at her, and Nancy Sue started bawling. The guests were completely shocked and embarrassed, and left as soon as they could.

Celine had gone into the child's room to quiet her down, and Carlos helped himself to more punch, eventually passing out on the sofa.

When he woke up, Celine and the baby were gone, and the house was dark. He looked outside and discovered their car was missing. He decided to call the police and ask them to put out a missing person's bulletin. Eventually, the police located his car in Houston, where Celine had returned to stay with her parents.

Celine filed for divorce in Houston. The citation published in the Daily Court Reporter in June of 1936 said, in part: "Defendant [Carlos] quarreled with plaintiff continually, complaining of almost everything she did, cursed and abused plaintiff, spoke of her to her friends in a most derogatory fashion, until further living together has been rendered insupportable." The divorce was granted in July, with Celine retaining custody of their child. Celine would later remarry, bear a second daughter, and live the rest of her life in Houston. Their daughter, Nancy Sue, was truly Carlos's daughter, the apple who didn't fall far from the tree. Later, while she was away in college, she played piano in bars to entertain her friends, drinking and having a wonderful time.

Her stepfather had to pay off her many bar bills when she graduated and would later cause her devoted parents to bemoan her several disastrous marriages.

CHAPTER FOURTEEN

1936—THE TEXAS PANHANDLE

Although Doris Sanders was born in Ada, Carlos's hometown, her family left there while she was a little girl. Her father, Joe, was a mechanic, and owned a garage. He got an offer to come to a small Texas town called Vega, a Spanish word meaning "meadow" in English, to set up shop rent-free in an existing warehouse building. The town needed a skilled mechanic, and Ada already had several, so he saw it as a chance to do better for his family. But Vega was anything but a meadow. Situated in Texas's arid panhandle, the nearest town of any size was Amarillo, thirty miles away, with a population of just over fifteen thousand. Vega's population was tiny, just about two hundred people. There were few girls of Doris's age, but she made fast friends with most of them, and they remained loyal to each other for years. There wasn't much to do in Vega. You had to be social, and it helped to be imaginative, as well. Doris was both.

As she blossomed into young womanhood, she was slender and attractive. Although her family couldn't afford extravagances, she was able to find things to wear that looked good and suited both her slim build and her lustrous dark brown hair and striking blue eyes. She had a sense of style in putting things together that complemented her features. She had no trouble attracting boys; the only problem being there were so few to choose from. Most were farm kids, and she wanted nothing to do with farms. In fact, she dreamed that someday she would meet some successful businessman or doctor or lawyer, and she would leave small town Texas forever.

The first step in her plan was to go to college and get a degree so she could improve her living conditions and opportunities. She didn't have many choices, however; the only school that made any sense for her, given her family's finances, was West Texas State Normal College in nearby Canyon, south of Amarillo. It would later become West Texas State Teachers College. There, she joined Beta Sigma Phi sorority and remained active in sorority affairs and events the remainder of her life. Although the choice of suitors expanded dramatically for her, she was selective in choosing who she would consider dating. She would decline invitations from anyone with a farming background, which was most young local male students. The students who didn't "have dirt under their fingernails," as she put it, were often young men who couldn't get into Texas Tech or one of the other nearby major institutions, usually because of laziness, poor grades, bad behavior, or some combination, and so had to settle for West Texas. Eliminating those from her dance card further narrowed her choices. However, among those remaining, most intended to enter the field of education, which was hardly the future she envisioned for herself. Finally, she just decided to wait and see what fate had in store for her. Maybe one day, something or someone unexpected would turn up.

Meanwhile, she nurtured her friendships in the sorority and joined in its activities. In her classes, she was a good student, getting average grades in the core curriculum. However, she did better than average in a few noncore courses, including an introduction to design and general business. Her no-nonsense demeanor impressed her business professors, and her intuitive grasp of design principles appealed to the design faculty. Her career counselors suggested that she might find a good fit in the fashion industry, which she felt was strongly appealing. The only problem was her lack of understanding about how to go about pursuing such a career. This was how things stood with Doris when she decided to accept an invitation from one young man who had passed her gauntlet of qualifications, to meet for drinks one night in Amarillo.

Meanwhile, Carlos was busy with Chevrolet, pitching their services and making sales calls throughout Texas. After one of these meetings, in Amarillo, Carlos dropped by the hotel bar early one chilly late fall evening. It was a bit crowded, and Carlos found a seat at the bar next to an attractive young woman. "Is this seat taken?" he asked.

"I was sort of saving it for a friend, but he's more than half an hour late, so help yourself," she said with a calibrated smile, not too warm, but not at all hostile. Doris had dressed for her no-show date in a sapphire blue dress that complemented her eyes and figure.

"I can't believe anyone would be so stupid or blind to stand you up," Carlos replied, as he sat down next to her. "My name is Carlos, Don Carlos Benson," he said.

"I'm Doris Sanders," she said, looking him straight in the eye but with a flush rising in her face.

Carlos caught the eye of the bartender and said, "We'd like to order, please." Then he turned to Doris and said, "What are you having, Doris?"

Still looking directly at him, she said, "I'll have a ginger ale."

Carlos turned back to the bartender and pulled a brown paper bag out of his briefcase, setting it down on the counter and sliding it toward the bartender. Much of Texas was still "dry," and customers had to buy their booze at package stores and then join "clubs" to get a mixed drink. "Two ginger ales and add a couple shots for each from the bottle here," he said.

As the barkeep turned away, Doris leaned closer and said in a whisper, "I'm not twenty-one yet, Carlos; they won't serve me."

"Just don't say a word, sweetie, you look plenty grown up. See, he thinks so too," he said, pointing at the bartender. Then he lowered his voice and asked, "So how old are you, Doris?"

"I'm nineteen. I'm a student over at West Texas State in Canyon," said Doris, quietly. "Do you know where that is?"

"Of course, I do. I'm a district representative for an automotive company, and my district covers every town in Texas. We're based in Dallas, but I travel a lot and I'm here for a district sales meeting."

"Oh, so you're from Dallas," Doris said, as the bartender served their drinks.

"Well, actually, I'm from Oklahoma originally—a little place you've probably never heard of, called Ada."

Doris was astonished. "That's where I was born! My father owned a garage there, Sanders Garage. My family used to live there, my parents and my four brothers and one sister."

"I know that place!" Carlos replied. "I've taken cars there to get repaired several times. I can't believe this!"

"How long has your family been there, Carlos?"

"Nearly since you were born, kiddo. My father was a US Marshal, based there, but who roved all around the Midwest as part of the liquor control board. I've got two sisters and two brothers, but only one sister is living in Oklahoma now. So, did you grow up in Ada?"

"No, we moved, and I grew up in Vega, not far from here."

"That's a pretty small town. I remember going with my father to a Masonic lodge meeting there."

"Yes, that's in the building where I went to school!" said Doris, excitedly as she smiled broadly. Her excitement grew partly from learning of these coincidences and partly from the bourbon in her drink. She liked this handsome stranger, so generous and pleasant.

"Doris," Carlos said, "if I can arrange it, would you care to meet me for dinner the next time I come through town? I feel I'd like to get to know you better, and maybe there are more surprises in store."

Doris drummed her fingers on the table, partly to hide her nervousness, and then nodded, saying, "Sure, that would be swell. I've really enjoyed getting to know you. Let me write down

my address and how to reach me by telephone; it's a little complicated." The flush was rising again on her face, as she dug in her
purse for a pen and a slip of paper.

When they parted after saying their goodbyes, Carlos walked
out of the lobby and into the chill night air, but he didn't feel it at
all; instead, he was elated. He knew there had been a spark in the
air between them. She made him feel lucky, and ten or fifteen years
younger.

CHAPTER FIFTEEN

1936 TO 1939—WITH DORIS IN DALLAS

So that's how Carlos happened to meet Doris, a young coed who attended college near Amarillo. Carlos arranged several more trips to Amarillo and staged a full-on campaign to woo Doris, not unlike the sales campaigns he had learned to wage selling automobiles. Only here there were no numbers of units sold to measure his progress, but only her smiles of appreciation, and hopefully soon more. This encouraged him to redouble his efforts, showering her with gifts and expensive dinners. Finally, one weekend, he brought her to Dallas, buying her clothing and accessories from Neiman Marcus, Titche-Goettinger, Sangers and A. Harris—it made her head spin, it was so exciting. When he suggested they spend the night at the Baker Hotel. She hesitated at first, but soon she was happy to accept. He bought her flowers and a new negligee for the occasion. None of the young boys she had dated could match him. He was so glamourous, handsome, and self-assured, and obviously had an especially important job—no small feat in an economy that was still recovering from the Depression years.

CHAPTER SIXTEEN

CHANGING FORTUNES, DETROIT 1938–1939

Meanwhile, Carlos was growing disenchanted with Chevrolet. Carlos didn't have Ed's patience, plodding away at the same old job with no promotions in sight and nothing exciting to look forward to. He felt stuck, and in late 1938, Carlos decided it was now or never, so he went to Detroit to talk about his future with Central Office. It soon became clear that he wasn't making any headway. While he was in Detroit absorbing this unwelcome information, he and Doris stayed with his brother, Ed. Ed's wife, Esther, was plainly unhappy with the arrangement, as the lifestyles of the childless couple did not fit well with a smoothly functioning family with young children, with set times for their activities.

CHAPTER SEVENTEEN

A CHANCE ENCOUNTER—DETROIT 1939

L ate in the 1930s, a group that became known as the Duquesne Spy Ring set up operations in the US to conduct sabotage and to collect information on America's manufacturing facilities and technological developments and to transmit that information to Nazi Germany. The group was headed by Frederick "Fritz" Duquesne, a naturalized US citizen originally from South Africa who had a long history of working clandestinely for Germany. One of Duquesne's agents was Heinrich Clausing, who became a naturalized US citizen in 1938. Clausing operated as a courier, assigned to find and deliver American automobile and aviation industry secrets. He established several contacts within the automotive industry, many of whom were unaware of his intentions to commit espionage.

One of Clausing's contacts was named Max Keller, a consultant for the auto industry in Detroit. Max was a gregarious fellow with sandy hair and distinctive red cheeks, who enjoyed making new acquaintances, often over drinks. One of these acquaintances was Carlos, who also enjoyed conversations over drinks. One evening in December, Carlos dropped by the Hotel LaSalle on his way back from GM's Central Office. There was an open seat at the bar, and he gladly took it, unbuttoning his damp overcoat and offering his hand to the fellow seated to his right.

"Howdy. I'm Don Carlos Benson. Were you saving this seat for someone?"

"Not at all. Make yourself comfortable. I'm Max Keller. Are you from around here, Carlos?"

Carlos replied, "No, actually I'm not. I'm visiting from Texas, just on a trip to my home office."

"What kind of work do you do that brings you up here from Texas?" asked Max.

"I'm an executive with Chevrolet," said Carlos." I run their operations in Texas, and I was just up here to straighten out some kinks in the supply chain."

"Oh, really?" Max said. "I run a shop that supplies production equipment and logistical advice to Fisher, GM's body works."

"You don't say!" said Carlos. "Well, then you'd understand. We have an inventory problem. Head office accountants are pushing this 'just in time' inventory as a means of tightening costs, but the unintended consequence is that any snags in inventory delivery results in bottlenecks that slow down delivery. That means we don't have enough cars to sell. So, they brought me up here to advise them on where to adjust controls, so the production doesn't bog down. They needed a practical, strategic overview of the whole process."

"Sounds like they got the right man for the job. Can I buy you a drink, Carlos?"

In fact, Carlos was not in Detroit as an advisor, but instead to ask for a promotion from district sales representative to regional sales manager, which he was denied. While he was there, he also signed up for Social Security, that new socialistic program that Roosevelt and his radical left-wing administration pushed through the rubber-stamp Congress. Although he hated the idea of a dole, he had to register sooner or later. As their conversation continued, Carlos found that Max agreed wholeheartedly that the Roosevelt administration was corrupt and power-hungry, put the country in grave danger, and was in thrall to George Meany's AFL-CIO.

"I tell you that Roosevelt wants nothing more than to go to war with Germany!" Max exclaimed. "That's what Lend Lease is all about—taking sides with the British," he said.

Daniel Brents

"I couldn't agree more!" said Carlos. "One thing I learned in Wilson's War is getting involved in Europe cost us plenty! I was wounded several times, and saw so many of my buddies die, for nothing! Furthermore, we probably chose the wrong side to fight against." It didn't trouble Carlos at all to stretch the truth about his wartime activities, especially if the result was to enhance his credibility.

"You know what, Carlos? You're a good egg. Let's have another drink and you can tell me how I can help with Chevy's production lines."

"Suits me, pal," said Carlos.

As the two continued to talk, Carlos spun more tales about his importance in the auto industry, his mastery of technologies with which he only had passing familiarity, and his disdain for the government. Max could hardly believe his good luck in running across this guy. He planned to keep tabs on Carlos and regularly get a high-level overview of the industry's capacity and weak points, exactly what the big boys in Berlin asked for when they tasked Clausen's team. Although the Germans paid well, they paid slowly, and it had been several months since Max's last payday. But this was perfect; the information was great, and this guy would spill for the cost of a few drinks – he liked to talk.

"Say, how long will you be in town, Carlos?", Max asked.

"Only two more days.", Carlos replied. "I have to get back to Texas quickly, before things go haywire there."

"Well, in that case, would you meet me again for drinks tomorrow afternoon? There's someone I would like you to meet."

"Sure," said Carlos, "as long as we can keep it brief. I still have to pack."

"That's no problem.", said Max. "I want to introduce you to my boss, Hank".

"Okay, sure thing.", said Carlos.

The following afternoon, the snow and slush were even worse than the day before, and Carlos arrived late at the LaSalle. Walking

64

over to the bar, he saw Max, talking with another guy. Max looked up and saw Carlos coming. He raised his hand and waved at Carlos.

"Carlos, over here.", said Max.

"So sorry I'm late.", Carlos said. "I'm not used to this miserable weather, and it held me up."

"That's okay," said Max. "Carlos, I'd like you to meet my boss, Hank Clausing, Carlos is the big shot from GM I was telling you about."

"Very pleased to meet you, Carlos. Max has filled me in on your production line issues and I'd like to think we could help. But first, what can we get you to drink?" said Hank.

"Thanks, Hank," said Carlos. "It's a pleasure to meet you too. I'll have a bourbon and soda."

"Coming right up!" said Hank as he waved at the bartender.

Just as Carlos removed his overcoat and the drinks were served, an attractive girl with a camera came up to Max and said, "Gentlemen, you fellows look happy. Can I take your photo to commemorate this friendly gathering?"

"You bet, honey," said Max. Turning to the other two men, he said, "Let's raise our glasses in a toast to smooth sailing, and she'll take our picture?"

The three of them smiled, raised and clinked their glasses, and Max said, "Down the hatch!" just after the flash went off. Max quickly dug in his pocket, pulled out some bills, and paid the photographer. "I'll send you fellas a print when I get them," he said, smiling broadly. In fact, Max had arranged for the photographer to come to them as soon as they were joined by Carlos. He wanted a record of this meeting, just in case.

Thus began a relationship that stoked Carlos's self-importance but would lie hidden in his background like a ticking time bomb.

But as the days turned to weeks, Carlos became more impatient and eventually disgusted. He couldn't fathom why Chevrolet didn't see his value and realize what a swell job he had been doing.

CHAPTER EIGHTEEN

GM CHANGES ITS MISSION AND CARLOS CHANGES EMPLOYERS

Everything had been working well for Carlos in the automotive industry until America entered World War II, but in 1942, "that Democrat son of a bitch Roosevelt" as Carlos called him, ordered the formation of the War Production Board, whose purpose was to convert the nation's industrial capacity from the production of consumer goods, including cars, to wartime materiel. During 1941, there were about three million automobiles that rolled off the production lines. That would come to a virtual halt in 1942. General Motors kept many of its sales managers, such as Ed, busy with the war effort, developing war drives and programs to boost production.

Carlos was a relative newcomer, a recent hire. Although he'd put in his time, he felt he wasn't getting anywhere. He'd made one trip to Detroit to try to convince them that if they didn't step up, he might no longer be available. When they disagreed about his value, he started looking around for something else.

As if there wasn't enough turbulence in his life, Carlos soon entertained and then accepted an offer to join Beasley Motors, the Oklahoma firm that handled multiple manufacturer's sales in the South-Central region, including several of GM's competitors, such as Dodge-Plymouth and Studebaker. His impatience soon led him to contact friends to introduce him to contacts at Studebaker, whose sales were struggling. He landed an executive sales position, but the timing could not have been worse for Carlos. Studebaker did not have GM's financial depth or resources, and Carlos, as one of the most recent hires, with few new cars to sell, was vulnerable. The Champion model was still being produced, in very limited quantities, with its 170-cubic-inch in-line six engine, and there was a "Blackout" model that was produced, that omitted any chrome-plated parts, as chrome was rationed. Nonetheless, new cars and parts were quite limited and soon became nonexistent.

In Carlos's mind, it was a lucky and enormous opportunity to step up from regional sales into upper management. In this new capacity, Carlos appeared at sales conferences and meetings throughout Texas, speaking about sales strategy and goals.

CHAPTER NINETEEN

CARLOS GETS A WARNING—DALLAS

I n October of 1941, Doris asked him to take her to the Texas State Fair again. She had a wonderful time last year, and this year was supposed to be even more spectacular. Carlos thought the fair was swell. He really liked the auto show, and Doris loved the Midway, with the rides, the crowds, the noise, the lights, and the excitement. It was one of the ways the twenty years age difference between them made itself apparent. They took the streetcars over to Fair Park, and the nearer they got, the more excited she became, talking faster, eyes sparkling, touching his arm, holding his hand, and fanning her face with the other. They walked down the Midway together, hand in hand. Doris's blue eyes glittered with excitement, and her voice rose over the noise. "Oh, Carlos! Should we take the Tilt-a-Whirl or the Ferris wheel? Or the Triple Racing Coaster?"

There was always fun food, like cotton candy and those new corny dogs. A Texas State Fair invention, these were sausages on a stick, covered in a fried cornbread batter. Swarms of kids, teenagers, and younger flowed from one site to the next, up and down the broad Midway. There were screams of terror and pleasure as the roller-coaster cars reached the apex and dropped like a bad dream, gathering steam until the bottom, only to slowly begin the climb again. There was also a concoction of intriguing smells whirling around, from cotton candy or floss, to popcorn, to the corny dogs.

Then there were the carnie shows, the geek shows, the freak shows, the shooting arcades and the stunt shows. It was tremendously exciting. He began thinking about his younger days when he and Jo Andrews began a romance. They had gone to the State Fair in Oklahoma City, and Carlos managed to hit the twenty-foot bell with the big hammer and won a kewpie doll for Jo, whom he still thought about so many years later. Thinking about Jo led him to mentally scroll through the subsequent chapters of his life, kind of like those peep shows on Deep Ellum (the lower part of Elm Street, in Dallas) where the flipping photos of girls stripping gave a sense of motion and excitement like a motion picture show. He thought about Bess when they lived in California, his second wife, Opal, and Celine. Jo had finally given up, she wasn't able to follow his many moves and her letters quit coming, but he thought of her at moments like this, that brought back memories of fun times when he was a kid and life was an open book.

Doris interrupted his reverie by excitedly pointing to a fortune-teller's tent. Doris didn't really believe in fortune tellers, and Carlos certainly didn't—he considered them all to be a waste of time and money. In any case, some phony couldn't tell him anything he didn't know already; he led a charmed life. But she insisted that they have their fortune told "to see if our dreams will come true," she said, with a laugh. Carlos's dreams were very big. He hoped one day to hit the jackpot, like winning a huge pot at poker. His upbringing was strict about gambling, just like it was about drinking. He didn't mind crossing the line though now that liquor was legal again, but he thought gambling was a matter of skill and luck. He did have big dreams, of a big house, expensive cars, fine clothes, and all the comforts. He wanted to make it big for Doris's sake, or his, so she would continue look up at him with admiration. And not just Doris, but somehow, he wanted it to impress Bess and Celine, and his parents and brothers and sisters too. And his daughters. He knew Doris would be thrilled to have money to burn, and he always had his eye out for a deal that could make his fortune—his big break. So, he entered the tent by her side, curious about what the gypsy would say.

Inside, it was stuffy and dark. Fortunately, they were in the middle of Indian Summer, when the weather takes a pleasant turn in

Texas after the brutal hot months. There was a waiting area with plain chairs and a few customers. A young girl dressed in a harem outfit gave them a card with a number in exchange for a half dollar, then told them to wait. They watched as the heavy curtain parted, and one client left and another went in as his number was called. He was a hayseed from the sticks, dressed in his best overalls, who slammed his straw hat back on as he scuttled out across the canvas floor. A nervous young woman came and went next, well-dressed, clutching her purse before her. Then a serious-looking youth, wearing a bowtie went in, wiping his hands on his trousers. He came out soon, wearing a wide grin, and it was their turn.

Beyond the curtain, the fortune teller was seated at an oval table, which rested on scattered oriental rugs. Chiffon nets were draped around the walls, and several smaller tables held lighted candlesticks. There were fat pillows scattered around the walls of the tent, and an incense burner smoked to the medium's left. She was dressed in oriental robes, and a large patterned shawl was draped over her head and shoulders. Her features were dark and sharp and her manner gentle. "Please be seated," she said with a heavy accent, which was difficult to place. They tried to make themselves comfortable in the stiff, caned chairs. A crystal globe was just to her right, on the table, but she never once referred to it. She studied them for a time, and then said to Doris, "May I take your hand, dear?" and reached over and took Doris by the wrist.

In a soft, barely audible voice, she told Doris that although there would be difficult days ahead in her life, she would be happy and comfortable. She told her that her work in a college sorority would provide very rewarding moments, and that she would end her days happily married but never have children of her own. Then she turned to Carlos and said, "And now, sir, may I have your hand?" She looked at his hand, then looked up at his eyes.

"You, sir, have had a turbulent life. Your father and mother are very important to you, and you try hard to earn their respect, although you don't always succeed. You are a very persuasive man, and this has served you well, although you continue to seek the type of work that is most meaningful and rewarding to you."

She paused for what seemed to be a long time. Then she said, "You will soon come to a time in your life when the outcome of your decisions may cause serious consequences for you and everyone who loves you. These will test your character and also your will. If you are true to what you know to be right and are honest with those who care for you, you can come through these dark times with renewed purpose and energy, and you will accomplish much.

"However," she said, "You have been impulsive and dishonest with yourself and others in the past, and it has cost you. If you do not change and follow the examples of your parents, remaining on a steady course and true to those who love you, you are in very great danger. I cannot say more than that."

Carlos was shaken by her warning, even though he was tempted to scoff at her words. They could apply to just about anybody. The reference to his dishonesty really hacked him off. He immediately rose, turned abruptly on his heel, knocking over his chair, and passed through the curtain. He pushed through the waiting area without a glance and then stopped outside the tent, deeply breathing in the air and blinking at the sunlight around him. Doris hurried to his side and asked if he was all right. "Carlos don't be upset," she said. It doesn't mean anything."

"Sure," he said, "I'm fine. She's just a babbling old hag. I just needed some air." Then he looked at her, grinned, and said, "Say, kid, let's go see if we can find a cold drink."

They had good years in Dallas and made trips back to Ada from time to time. In 1940, not long after they were married, Carlos took Doris there for a family Christmas reunion with Mother, his sister Maude and her daughter Marjorie, sister Belle and her daughter Lila June, brother Max and his wife, Billie, and their son Tom Ed. Max, still stung by the fact that his younger brother was given his father's name instead of him, preempted Ed by giving his firstborn son their father's name. Everyone dressed in their best.

Carlos wore his three-piece suit and his usual smug, self-satisfied expression. Doris, however, looked uncomfortable. She felt like she was an intruder and constantly looked over at Carlos for reassurance. However, he was too absorbed with family dynamics to pay attention to her discomfort. Max, envious of his brother's apparently successful life and career, noticed Carlos's attention was elsewhere, and as they came back in the house from the final photo, Max pulled Doris aside and said, "Welcome to the family, Doris. I wish only the best for you both. You know, Carlos has a history of treating women like sticks of chewing gum. He chews on them for a while, and when he gets tired of them, he spits them out." Then Max left her side.

Doris, distressed and on the verge of tears, immediately went to Carlos and pulled him aside. "What did he mean about that?" she asked Carlos, for Carlos had told her nothing about previous romances. Carlos was furious that Max had opened this can of worms, and after minimizing what Max meant and reassuring Doris, He confronted his brother keeping his voice down so that their mother wouldn't hear him.

"You son of a bitch," Carlos said. "You deliberately said that to upset her and embarrass me."

Max shrugged this off, claiming that he thought Doris had already been told everything by Carlos. "Maybe so, but you had no right to take that on yourself," Carlos spat. Whereupon Carlos turned on his heel and went back to Doris. "C'mon, babe, let's leave this place. I've got important matters in Dallas that I have to get back to." And so went Doris's introduction into the family.

When they returned to Dallas, they began to have problems. Doris pressed Carlos about his previous relationships and learned that she was his fourth wife. She was shocked and distressed that he had hidden this from her. Meanwhile, her persistent questions made Carlos embarrassed and angry. He was too involved in his future to dwell on his uncomfortable past. Sure, he had made a few mistakes, but here he was, successful, doing his best to take care of her and make their future more secure.

CHAPTER TWENTY

1942 TO 1945—DALLAS AND JACKSON, MISSISSIPPI

He redoubled his efforts in regional sales at Studebaker without success, but because of the war and hampered production, he finally succumbed to the temptation of padding his sales reports back to the home office. He arranged with a group of friends to purchase cars, wait until the close of the reporting period, and then bring the cars back to their dealers before payments were due. His boss at the home office recognized this game and called him in for a dressing down. After making him wait outside for an hour and a half, his boss finally buzzed him on the squawk box. "Get your butt in here, Carlos." Carlos entered and his boss said, "Close the door, Carlos.". Then his boss raised his voice and said, "Carlos, you dope! Who do you think you're kidding? You think we were born yesterday? You and four other regional sales managers pulled the same stunt, and the only reason you're not getting the sack right now is that we can't afford to lose all four of you at the same time. Not yet anyway! I went way out on a limb and saved your sorry ass this time. It won't happen again! Now straighten up and fly right or you're history!"

But as the war dragged on, it was clear that the automotive industry was not going to recover any time soon. It was no longar his pathway to the top, and after the second cut in his salary, he started looking for something else. He went to Detroit again, to see if any of the other manufacturers were hiring. He and Doris stayed again with his brother, Ed and his wife, Esther, and their young son, Tommy. None of the car manufacturers were hiring, but he did manage to find an opening at Fruehauf Trailer Company. The job was based in Jackson, Mississippi, but that was okay, and the money would be good enough. After two weeks, he and Doris had worn out their welcome at his brother's little home, and Esther started throwing around hints that she could use some help picking up, preparing meals, and running errands. They got the message and took the train back down to Dallas, to arrange their move to Jackson.

Once they moved and he started his new job, however, Carlos found that working for an equipment company was not so glamorous. He missed the excitement of automobiles, with their new models and snazzy designs. Jackson's population was just 62,000, while Dallas was nearly 300,000 and growing. The ambiance just wasn't the comparable. Jackson was a sleepy burg, somehow still stuck in the days of the Civil War, and things there seemed so backward. It was mainly an agricultural center, which worked fine for Fruehauf, but less so for Carlos and Doris. There were many more Negroes, and many of the white people lacked education or their wives were uninterested in things that interested Doris. Everyone there but them seemed they came from the sticks. They had virtually no social life together. Carlos put together a poker group, and Doris tried to form a similar bridge group. However, bridge wasn't as popular with women as poker was for the men, and she found it impossible to get a foursome together for any length of time.

Carlos was doing quite well at poker, repeating the strategies he had employed in Austin some years ago. Most of the guys in the group were not the swiftest bunnies in the woods, and he quickly learned their "tells," the little habits that telegraphed their emotional state and intentions. Several were in banking, and although the industry was quite sleepy in Jackson and not very demanding, it paid well. A few were store owners. At first, the men and their wives would gather just to be sociable. They would sing "Shine on Harvest Moon" and other songs of the times over drinks (called toddies or highballs) well into the night. While one of the wives played the piano, Carlos would join in with his trumpet. All had money; it was the first prerequisite that Carlos used when putting his group together. During the time they were in Jackson, Carlos was making almost as much from poker as from his job with Fruehauf.

Meanwhile, despite the social gatherings, Doris was growing increasingly restive and unhappy in Jackson; it was so different than what she was used to, and the life they had before, in Dallas. Carlos remembered how the moves and living in uninteresting places affected Celine, and he was determined not to play that hand again. So, although he was raking in good dough in his present situation, he started looking for something back in Dallas. Eventually, exaggerating his prior real estate experience in Tulsa and Galveston, he was hired at Pan American, a Dallas real estate and insurance agency. The money could be pretty good, although he was on commission, and he really had to hustle. They moved into a rental place near Southern Methodist University, and then, using their savings from Mississippi, they found a duplex for sale in University Park, a swanky suburb that was surrounded by Dallas, but close into town. It was perfect; they could live on the first floor and rent out the floor above. Working on commissions was okay, and at first, he landed some big sales. But as the war went on and on, the big ones began to dry up, and he started having trouble making ends meet. Doris got a job as a secretary, but still they were just scraping by.

CHAPTER TWENTY-ONE

THE MEET-UP, DALLAS 1944

J ust then in 1944, after years of tracking, at last Max Keller got wind of Carlos's trail. When they last met, Carlos had said he was from Texas. Max wasn't sure he remembered Don Carlos's last name, something like Bentson or Benton. He concentrated on the big cities: Houston, Dallas, San Antonio, Austin, Ft. Worth. He knew Carlos was with Chevrolet, so he would call their offices in those places, asking for Carlos Benton and then Carlos Branson and Don Benton, but he wasn't getting anywhere. Then it occurred to him that Carlos may have gone to work for Ford, Chrysler, or Hudson—one of the other major manufacturers. Still no luck. Then he tried back in Detroit, following the same trails, with no results. At last, he had a brainstorm. Remembering that Carlos had been visiting from Dallas when they met, Max went to the public library there and looked in the City Directory. At the time, it was common that publishing companies would print directories that listed the names and work addresses of businesses and businesspeople. And there he found it: a listing for Carlos Benson, who worked for Pan American Brokerage in Dallas. Max recognized the name Benson, but he found it odd that Carlos had apparently left the auto industry for real estate; still there was no mistaking the name. All that remained was to track him down and confirm that this was the same guy.

Max called Pan American and asked to speak with Carlos Benson. A few seconds later, Carlos picked up and said, "This is Carlos. Who's calling please?"

"Mr. Benson, this is Charles Norsby," said Keller. "Your name was given to me by a neighbor of yours, on...let's see...what was the name of that street...?" Max said as he loudly shuffled some papers.

"Was it Rosedale?" asked Carlos.

"Found it, that's right, Rosedale!" said Max. "This neighbor said you have a good knowledge of available real estate in the area, and I'm wondering if we could meet to discuss that."

"Sure," said Carlos. "Just let me check my appointments." After a brief pause, while Carlos inspected his fingernails, he said, "I have an hour free tomorrow at 3:00 p.m. Would that work for you?"

"Certainly," said Max. "But I'm just visiting in town, so I wonder if we could meet at my hotel. I'm staying at the Adolphus, downtown. Would that be okay?"

"Yeah, sure," said Carlos. "What room number?"

"Room 402; but you can just ask for me by name at the front desk. Again, I'm Charles Norsby."

"I've got it, Mr. Norsby. I'll see you at three sharp," said Carlos.

"Swell, I look forward to it," said Max, and hung up.

Next, Max looked up the address for Pan American. It was in the Southland Life building, very near the Adolphus. He went outside, hailed a taxi, and said, "How much for the rest of the day?" They agreed on a price, and Max told the cabbie to drive to the Southland Life building, where Pan American had their offices. He told the cabbie he was a private investigator, hired to follow a guy by his jealous wife, and to park so that they could spot the target without being seen, and follow him when he came out of the building. It was 4:30 when they got there, and at 5:15, Max spotted Carlos as he emerged from the front doorway. "There he is, the guy wearing the gray hat!" said Max, excitedly. "Don't lose him and there's an extra five bucks in it for you."

Carlos walked down Commerce Street and turned right on Lane Street and ducked into a bar about midway down the block. "Uh-huh, that figures," muttered Max. "Okay, same MO. We wait here until he comes back out and we follow him again."

This time, they waited over an hour. When Carlos came out, he walked back to Commerce Street. He caught the Highland Park–Southern Methodist trolley headed north, and the cab and its passenger followed. After making a transfer to a University Park line, Carlos pulled the cord and stepped down at Rosedale Boulevard, walking the short distance up the block to his home, at 3516. Max was very excited. The "park Cities" were swanky locations, and that meant Carlos was probably in the chips.

He leaned over the seat and said to the driver, "Listen, can you do me a favor? I want you to go up to the door, knock, and ask for directions somewhere, I don't care where, come back, and tell me what you see and hear, okay? There's another five bucks in it for you if you do a good job. I want to know if he's with his wife, and what they say to each other. I want to know what the furniture looks like, how she's dressed, everything. Hang around as long as you can, play a little dumb to spend time, but nothing obvious. See if there's any mail, and if so, see who it's from and addressed to.

"Okay," the cabbie said, as he pushed some newspapers aside in the front seat and then exited the cab. He went up to the door, knocked, and it was answered by a woman. There was some back and forth, and then Carlos appeared in the foyer and talked with the cabbie. Carlos became more animated and then the cabbie tipped his hat and backed away. He came back to the cab and Max. "Well, that was interesting," said the cabbie. "I must have interrupted some big damn quarrel 'cause they were going at it tooth and nail when I walked up. She pulled herself together and spoke more normal, but he was still giving her hell. You asked how she was dressed; she was dressed to the nines, really a swanky dame, good figure too. There was mail on the table next to the door, but I couldn't read nothing but a first name on a Neiman's bill. It was addressed to Mrs. Doris."

"Okay, you did good," said Max. Actually, he was very pleased with the information. "Let's go back to the Adolphus now."

CHAPTER TWENTY-TWO

CONSEQUENCES

The next day, just before 3:00 p.m., Carlos entered the Adolphus hotel lobby. He had only gone a few steps inside when a voice nearby said, "Carlos?"

Carlos turned and said in surprise, "Max? Max Keller! What are you doing here?"

"I'm also known as Charles Norsby, Carlos. Why don't we sit down over here, and I'll explain everything."

"What the hell is this?" Carlos said. "What the hell are you up to?" He resisted Max's tug on his arm.

"If you'll just calm down a little bit, I'll explain it all," said Max, leading Carlos over to a lobby chair.

When the two were seated, Max said to Carlos, "I had a hell of a time tracking you down, Carlos. I thought you worked for GM. By the way, would you like a cigarette?"

"Yeah, thanks. I just don't understand. What's with the Charles Norsby act? What are you really up to?" asked Carlos.

Max lit their cigarettes, blew out his match with a cloud of smoke, and said, "I can't blame you for being surprised, Carlos. It's been a while since we last talked."

"Yeah, about GM, I left them and went with Studebaker, but then Roosevelt closed down auto production, so I had to find something else. I had a brief stint with Fruehauf in Mississippi but didn't like it and left. I had some experience with real estate, so I got on with Pan American."

"No wonder we lost contact," said Max, "you've been a busy boy. But apparently, you're doing okay, and landed on your feet. That's a swell place you have in University Park."

"How do you know where I live? What is this?" asked Carlos.

"I know lots of things about you, Carlos," said Max. "I know you're married; I know about Doris." Then Max took a chance by adding, "I know the two of you are having trouble getting along, and that she's a big spender."

"So, what's it to you, Max? For the last time, what's this all about?" said Carlos, rising from his chair.

"Hold on, hold on, will you? You're going to want to hear me out, Carlos," said Max. "Remember all that info about auto production that you and I talked about back in '39 and '40? Remember how we talked about kinks in the supply chains, and metallurgy and sources of rubber for tires? Well guess what? My boss, who you met, was really interested in all that stuff. And he passed it all on to another interested party. And guess who that was, Carlos?" Max paused, giving Carlos a chance to answer.

"How would I know? What are you talking about? Ford? Or Chrysler?"

"No, Carlos. I'm talking about Germany, Nazi Germany."

Carlos was stunned. "That's crazy! It's impossible! That's a goddamned lie!" said Carlos.

"No, that's the sad truth. And remember, you met my boss in Detroit one night, just before you came back to Texas. In fact, I have a photograph of the two of you, toasting each other at the bar, remember? I had the girl photograph just the two of you."

At this, Carlos felt an icy-cold lump in the pit of his stomach, like a lead weight, growing in size, getting heavier, as the real purpose of the meeting began to dawn on him.

"Now what you may not know is that Hank, my boss, was part of the Duquesne Spy Ring, that got rolled up by the FBI in '42. And Hank got rolled up with them. He's still in the clinker. He got eight years and he's still doing time. Fortunately, for me at least, he didn't mention my role in all this, so I've been lucky. Luckier than you, in fact."

"What do you mean?" said Carlos. "I had nothing to do with all that!"

"Maybe not, Carlos, but you wouldn't know that if you saw this photo. In fact, it might look like you were pretty deeply involved."

Carlos snatched the photo out of Max's hands and ripped it into pieces. "But nobody's going to see this photo now!" he said.

"You think that's the only copy, Carlos? Don't you remember I told the girl to send me three copies, so we could each have one. You just tore up your copy, but I have two more, locked safely away."

Carlos groaned and said, "Okay, what do you want, Max?"

"I'm sure the FBI or the Times Herald here would be interested in the photos, but I'll go easy on you, Carlos. I'll only charge you five thousand—each."

This time, Carlos felt as though the weight in his stomach was instead a blow, and he doubled over in pain. "Ten thousand!" he gasped. "How do you think I could get that much dough?"

"I don't know, Carlos. Use your imagination. Your home maybe or your car or your old age savings; you tell me."

Carlos replied, "I don't have anywhere near that kind of ready cash. Can I take some time to come up with the dough?"

"Sure," said Max. "Just wire me a thousand by next Friday, and another thousand each month, and I'll send one photo when you've reached five, and the other photo when you're reached ten."

"And the negative!" said Carlos.

"And the negative," said Max.

"You son of a bitch!" said Carlos.

"You might want to watch your language, Carlos. We're joined at the hip now, like those Siamese twins, in the freakshow. And if the least little thing happens to me, you'll feel it too, right away. Those photos will go straight to J. Edgar that's all" said Keller, referring to J. Edgar Hoover, the head of the FBI. "Here's the instructions on how to wire the money. On Friday, right?"

Although the war in Europe looked like it was nearing the end, the nation remained at war with Japan, and automobile production was still halted for the foreseeable future. His prospects weren't likely to improve anytime soon. *"Now this! Blackmail!"* His self-assurance had suffered a blow, and like what happened between him and Celine, his relationship with Doris had suffered, as well. She hated insecurity, and losing his job at Studebaker had made her feel very insecure. Lady luck had turned on him. *Just like a woman*, he thought. He felt increasingly cornered, which affected his job performance, making matters worse. As he reviewed his career, he felt victimized by events out of his control, by women who failed him, by responsibilities he never asked for, and by bosses who were unreasonable. And on top of it all, a blackmailer! There was no doubt that things were going from bad to worse and he was frustrated, fearful, and very angry.

CHAPTER TWENTY-THREE

FRIDAY, MAY 4, 1945 4:10 P.M. CWT—DALLAS

"Come in, Carlos. Close the door."

Carlos didn't like the looks of this setup; he'd heard these words before, and they always preceded bad news. "Close the door" likely meant that a door was about to close for him. Good thing he had slipped his coat back on. He immediately tried to steer the conversation in the direction of sunlight.

"Say, Chaz, that's a swell tie you're wearing. I almost bought one just like it myself, but while the mug in the department store was making his pitch, this skirt walked by, and I left him with that tie hanging in the air."

"Carlos."

"I followed her down the aisle and she stopped for a moment at the perfume counter, and then she looked back at me. Then she swooshed away again, and before I knew it, I was on the street, walking beside her, and she wouldn't look at me, but she was smiling."

"Carlos."

"We walked down to the end of the block..."

"Goddammit, Carlos, be quiet a minute!"

"You think maybe I should have bought the tie?"

"For Christ's sake, Carlos, I'm trying to talk with you about something important! You're an ace at getting sidetracked, and as a goddamn matter of fact, that's what I want to talk to you about!" Charles, or "Chaz," as only Carlos called him, was getting nervous, and it fed his anger.

Daniel Brents

"Well come on, Chaz, you know I'm always glad to hear whatever you have to say, because even though I might be pretty swell at sales, you wrote the book, as far as I'm concerned. In fact, when I was back at Regional last month, I was telling the guys..."

"Goddammit, Carlos, shut up a minute, will you?"

This finally had the desired effect. Rolling two pencils together on Charles's glass-topped desk, Carlos said, "Okay, Chaz, sure, whatever you say; I'm sorry. What's up?"

Charles would have been more patient, and more kind, if Carlos hadn't interrupted him so much. The problem was, the guy was so likeable and glib that it was hard to be tough on him, even if his performance was dragging. But Charles was getting pressure, and he really had no choice. Carlos's diversions only made it worse, and the pressure of what he had to do and the nervousness he felt finally erupted, once he finally had Carlos's attention, and he blurted out, "Carlos, you're fired!"

No stranger to this scene, Carlos immediately rose out of his seat to gain height over his boss, grimaced, placed his hands palms down on the desk in front of him, wrinkled his brow, and countered, "Now, Chaz, before you say something we'll both regret, let's calm down and talk this over. You don't want to do something rash, so let's talk this through." Carlos began pacing back and forth, gesturing. "If we can work out a plan together, I'm sure we can hit the numbers we set together, and I've been giving this a lot of thought. I have a new slant on how we can make a fresh campaign that can bring in more sales in only a few months; I just need to get your help on refining the plan, given your razor-sharp views on sales promotion."

"Carlos, we've had this conversation, at least five times. I can't seem to get through to you! It's over! You can't hit your numbers, and I can't look the other way anymore! I'm getting pressure from upstairs to produce, and you're not bringing in any real clients—just guys you meet somewhere on the street that haven't got two nickels to rub together. Your draw is more than you're bringing in, and we've given you so many advances on commissions that haven't come through, that we've just got to call it quits."

Sensing a glimmer of an opening, or at least maybe a sympathetic ear, Carlos, dropped his voice and said, "Boss, can't we talk this through?" Starting slowly, but building, Carlos said, "I know you've got pressure, but the goddamned war is gumming up the works, and now that the Nazis are almost licked, it'll soon be over. If we can just ride out a few more months, things will turn around, the GI's will be coming home, and all hell will break loose! There will be new families, new homes, new cars, new policies, new investments, new everything! We're going to have a fabulous year! By December, there'll be no looking back! Come on! Take the long view! It's going to turn up roses, and together we can ride the wave to the top! Just work with me a little while longer and we can prove that the world has changed for the better! You need me with you when you get there! I can help take you there. You've got to believe in me!"

But Chaz didn't, not anymore. He remained silent, staring at Carlos, and his silence said he had said all he was going to say.

To cover his embarrassment, rather than collecting his things from his desk, Carlos walked straight out. Even the pictures of his wife and his mother and father were left behind. He would call Jimmy Thompson tomorrow to collect them for him and bring them by on Monday night. What a Friday! It was a goddamned weekend, and it was going to be hell. Doris would not be happy. This was the third, no the fourth, job he had lost since they'd been married, and he could hear her bitching already. The time, after Studebaker fell through, he thought she would never quit—never quit screeching at him about what a loser he was. She started sniping about him with his family, too, and that was murder.

He couldn't go home. It was only 4:30, and she wouldn't be back from work for another hour, but he just couldn't face the conversation to come. One thing he knew, he would keep leaving the house in the mornings, pretending to go to work, until he could figure something out or find a new job. He decided he would go have a drink and think about what to do.

CHAPTER TWENTY-FOUR

TUESDAY, MAY 8, 1945 8:15 P.M. CWT—DALLAS

"It had to be you, it had to be you,
"I wandered around, and finally found, somebody who,
"Could make me be true, could make me be blue,"

The song played through her mind as she scrubbed the dinner dishes. She sang with the radio:

"For nobody else, gave me a thrill, with all your faults, I love you still,
"It had to be you, wonderful you,
"It had to be you."

Doris was thrilled, delirious with joy. It was her birthday, and earlier this morning, the Allies had announced Germany's surrender. The war in Europe was over, at long last. Who could ask for a better birthday present?

Life was going to turn up roses, she was sure. She had a good job. It wasn't important like Carlos's job, she readily admitted, but it was steady, and she liked it at the insurance company. She liked her boss, Mr. Grover, and the girls with whom she worked as a secretary there at Paramount. Dallas was home, not her real home, but way better than the vast and empty Panhandle, better than Amarillo. She had been here for several years, and it was bustling—you could just sense that it was an up-and-coming town. It was nothing like

Jackson, and there was nothing like it back in the Panhandle; she thought of it more like Los Angeles, where her father had gone to work as a mechanic in an aircraft factory—just a little smaller. It was spread out like LA, but it had nice suburbs and more affordable places to live. She liked living in University Park. She really loved it when she told someone where she lived, and she saw their eyes widen and their eyebrows lift slightly. Doris and Carlos lived in one of the smaller houses on the block, a duplex, and at sixteen years, it wasn't as new or as big as most of the others, but it suited their needs. It was really a swanky area, and although it was a stretch to buy it a couple years ago, Carlos was earning $2,000 to $2,500 depending on commissions, and with her $525 and the income from renting the upstairs apartment, the mortgage of $70 a month was just a bit more than a quarter of their combined income. Carlos said they should live up to their aspirations and she agreed; anyway, it was convenient to downtown. Carlos didn't share much information with her about their finances, but in spite of all of his career changes, he seemed so confident of everything that she didn't feel any need to question it.

She loved working downtown. There was the Mayflower doughnut shop on the corner of Ervay and Live Oak where she would get a snack to take to the office. She loved the place, with light coming in from two sides, the bustle, the smell of fresh coffee and doughnuts, the clatter of dishes, and the illustration of the "Optimist's Creed" poem on the wall:

She was an optimist herself and believed that no matter how challenging things may seem, there was always a rainbow just over the horizon. It was a little challenging lately, but nothing a new pair of shoes couldn't overcome.

And there was a great little barbeque place down on Commerce, with sawdust on the floor, and you could sit in school chairs to eat your sandwich at lunchtime. On the way back you could window shop at Titche's, A. Harris, Sanger's, or Neiman's. She would visit with some girl friends from the office, and even plan to come back after work, before catching the trolley back home. Carlos would usually come back later in the evening, after his business meetings and sales calls. He worked really hard, and it was disappointing that some of his bosses and clients didn't always recognize or appreciate his abilities as much as they should. Still, they were doing okay, and he said things were looking up. She had to look nice for her job, and she found wonderful new dress styles at the downtown stores. However, there were some storm clouds over the horizon because their relationship was growing more stressful. Carlos didn't talk about it much, but sometimes he would lash out at her with a fury that was surprising and, she felt, completely undeserved. They had started fighting, but she was an eternal optimist, certain that things would work out if they just stuck to first principles and stayed loyal to each other. But how could anyone not be excited that at last, the long war with the Nazis was over, and that we had won so decisively. She just wished that Carlos was here now right now to share the moment.

On this night, however, Carlos was later coming home than usual, and she had eaten without him. The smell of bacon still hung in the air. She was starting to get worried when he finally burst in, carrying a huge bouquet of flowers, threw his hat down on the sofa, and presented them with a flourish, saying: "Let's celebrate, Doris, honey! I've got news! Big news!"

She was happy with his good cheer. "Bigger than the end of the war?" she asked. He understood that the war was necessary, but he hated it all the same. And he replied, "Yes, even bigger than the end of the goddamned war. It's the beginning of a new chapter in our lives!" Doris searched for a vase for the flowers as he said excitedly, "I had a meeting this evening with a business friend who was talking about how things are going to change, once the war's over. He said that car sales are going to be the wave of the future, because now wartime production will shift back to cars, and because of all the growth that will come as the GI's return home and the economy changes to a peacetime footing—just like after the first war, but better. He said he wished they could find someone with sales experience in the automotive industry, but no one they've talked to has the right background.

"'Well,' I said, 'How about someone who was a sales executive with Chevrolet, Ford, and Studebaker?' And he said, 'If I knew someone like that, I'd hire them on the spot!' So, long story short, he offered me a top position as a transportation sales engineer at an up-and-coming company here in Dallas, one of the top auto parts companies in the nation! He told me they need someone like me with experience in the automotive world, because that's the heart of their business. Everyone knows cars are the way America will move in the future, and they want to capitalize on it, so he said they desperately need me to help them integrate that know-how into their business plan!"

"Oh, Carlos, that's so wonderful!" she said. But he barreled on.

"So, I called Chaz up and told him that as much as I have enjoyed working there at Pan American, this was something that was in my blood, and I had to seize this opportunity! This is the future! I'm joining the Whelan Company to manage their parts sales in Louisiana, Texas, Arkansas, and Oklahoma! Can you imagine how the world will change once the war ends? Everyone will need cars. Everyone will need roads and bridges! Rail will expand, and air, too, but especially cars! It's going to be the biggest transformation our country has ever seen, and as much as I've enjoyed working in the brokerage, this is the future and I have to be part of it! Chaz couldn't argue with that! So go get your hat and things and let's go out to celebrate the occasion!"

Excited by his enthusiasm, Doris ran into the bedroom and freshened up her makeup. Grabbing her hat and hurrying down the hallway, the song in her mind was one of Carlos's favorites, "Blue Skies."

Carlos was actually on the edge of terror. After all, Whelan was just a car parts company, with none of the excitement or the big money in sales that he had experienced before the war. But he needed a job, any job, not least to make blackmail payments. His several personal crises seemed so overwhelming, and he was desperate to escape them. He didn't like inflicting pain on Doris, but sometimes she pushed him too far. He had to admit, she wasn't entirely aware of the potential threats he faced. He hadn't felt it would be right to bring her completely into the picture; rather, it was his duty to protect her from the dangers they faced. Similarly, he absolutely did not want to cause pain or embarrassment to his mother by sharing his problems with her. He wanted her to be proud of him, not worry about him. During his last divorce, he had been too ready to unload his problems on Celine, and she had complained bitterly of his mental harassment. He had only shared his unhappiness because he felt she should be clear-eyed about the conflict she was creating with her bitching about all the moves. As it turned out, he had reacted too strongly, often acting injured while causing injury. He knew that now, and besides, he needed some source of income and to avoid the same consequences with Doris.

As usual, Carlos had chosen to describe this opportunity in the most positive and optimistic light, as much to convince himself as Doris. Maybe even stretching the facts a bit while glossing over or omitting a few details, why not? The H. H. Whelan Company was an auto accessories wholesale company, founded in Dallas by Harry Whelan in the 1930s. The company sold parts to dealers and repair shops. Carlos had experience and contacts throughout the region that might be helpful, but once again, he would be on commissions, and it would be tough to make ends meet, especially with Max Keller's threat looming over his head. Besides, he needed a source of income, if only to hit he tables so he could get ahead again.

Several months in a row they had a hard time making their mortgage payment, and there was just no money for extras, the way there used to be. He was worried and anxious, and when that happened, his temper was short. He didn't see how things could get any worse, and then she would come home with piles of new dresses and shoes.

"Goddammit, Doris, take them all back!" he yelled. "You can't keep spending money like it's water!"

"It's my own money and I can do what I want with it!" she said. "If you don't like it, why don't you find another job that pays more!"

It was all Carlos could do to keep from punching her in the face. Instead, he clenched his fists and stalked away, while tears of frustration streaked down Doris's cheeks. Soon, she could hear him throwing things in the kitchen.

He never thought of explaining or apologizing for their changed circumstances. He was too frustrated and angry to sympathize with her. Instead, he felt she was deliberately trying to undermine him. He was unable to open up to her and share the burdens he was carrying. Instead, he would yell at her and tell her to take her purchases back. Not understanding the seriousness of the pressures he was facing, she would say spiteful things and they would spiral into a shouting match. He and Doris had quarreled more and more. Often it would be about something trivial, such as a new recipe she tried and he didn't like and was too honest about his lack of approval, or when she asked him to clean up in the bathroom after shaving. It seemed they were often at odds, and the bad mood and bitterness affected his work. It was hard to be upbeat and maintain a glib demeanor when his problems were eating at him. He knew he was in a downward spin, and the only relief he found was when he drank, which only made his behavior more erratic and unreliable. Finally, just slightly less than a month after taking his new job, he and Doris had a huge fight about overdue bills, and they both said things they knew crossed the line. Neither of them held back. He was being deliberately mean and unreasonable. She was uncooperative and uncaring and a spendthrift. She broke down crying, and then left the house to meet a friend and to try to get her mind off Carlos and her deeply disturbed feelings. Carlos, meanwhile, was in a black mood, angry, hurt, depressed, and uncertain about his future. A few days ago, he was uncertain about the coming weeks. Now, he was uncertain about the coming hours. He had fallen so far! At one point, he was on top of the world, with a family, a prestigious job, and a bright future. Now, it had all come crashing down.

CHAPTER TWENTY-FIVE

DALLAS, 1940 TO 1944

At the time Carlos and Doris lived in Dallas, the city was plagued by corrupt government, underworld gambling, and crime.

From a book[4] about Dallas gambling kingpin Benny Binion:

DURING THE WAR years, gambling in Dallas became so flagrant that city officials, determined not to enforce anti-gambling laws, were often hard-pressed to avoid stumbling on it accidentally. Every downtown hotel, with the possible exception of the Baker and the Adolphus, was home to at least a regular crap game, if not a full-fledged casino. Benny Binion's Southland Group ran the gambling at the Southland, the Blue Bonnet, and the St. George, along with several other lesser operations. In his historic interview with the University of Nevada Oral History Program, Binion described the downtown scene this way: "Well, [the games] were in hotel suites, you know. We'd just have a big suite of rooms have the tables in there, have a bar, and we'd send out to different restaurants and get the food.

... Gambling in all its forms (except at the local race tracks) was, of course, illegal in Dallas, but an accommodation reached with local authorities even before the

---

[4] *I'll Do My Own Damn Killing* (pp. 59-60, 61-62). Sleeper, Gary, Barricade Books. Kindle Edition.

war insured that the casinos operated with little or no meaningful official interference.

The population of Dallas grew rapidly with the oil boom of the early 1930s, and the growth continued through the Depression as farmers abandoned the land and moved to the cities. From 1930 to 1950, the city's population nearly doubled, from 260,000 to 434,000, and the area grew from 40 square miles to more than 110. Government struggled to cope with this growth and the resulting increase in demand for city and county services.

In the hope of averting a potential financial crisis, city and county officials hit upon a scheme to "tax" illegal gambling by conducting periodic raids and levying fines for misdemeanor gambling violations. The resulting gambling tariff generated as much as $200,000 per year in city and county revenues, and Binion estimated that, over the years, he personally paid $600,000 in gambling fines. Of course, this system of illegally licensed gambling infuriated the segment of the population Benny called "the do-gooders and Bible-thumpers," and occasional sweeping raids were necessary at times to appease the more law-abiding folk.

Carlos had not intended to get sucked in, but his money problems became more and more desperate, and he considered how he might dig himself out of the hole that was getting deeper and deeper. He had, of course, heard about the gambling and the kingpins behind it, but had steered clear of it; his poker skills were good but maybe not good enough to sidestep risk. It all started innocently enough when he accompanied a friend, Nick Manno, to catch the action at the Southland Hotel one night. Nick's cousin worked there and could get them in. They were just going to have a few drinks, see what went on, and then leave.

They met in front of the Melba Theater on Elm Street, then walked the short block and a half to Main Street, where the hotel was located in a plain, brown brick box of a building. Crossing the lobby, they climbed the stairs to the mezzanine, headed for room 226, and pressed a button next to a door marked Private. Nick's cousin Tony slid open a speakeasy-style window and unlocked the door. Beyond, the room was full of smoke, noise, talk, laughter, and shouting, and the clatter of dice and chips. They walked over to the bar and ordered drinks—nothing complicated, just bourbon and scotch and mixers. Then Tony walked them over to one of the eight-foot tables where there was just enough room for them. Tony explained that they were expected to place a bet, or they would have to leave. Nick had probably been aware of the requirement after arranging the visit with his cousin. Carlos was surprised but was unwilling to lose face in the crowd, so he played along, putting a fin (five dollars) down on the table and buying the house minimum, one chip. He put it on the Pass Line, and was happy to see that after the throw, his money had doubled when the shooter rolled a seven. He decided to leave the chips where they lay, and this time, the shooter rolled eleven, and Carlos's bet was doubled again. Carlos began to relax and have fun. Within the next hour, he had won $520 on an original bet of five dollars. But he became nervous again and decided to quit for the night, cashed in his chips, and told Nick he was headed home. *What a terrific night; I really did okay! I was smart to quit while I was ahead. Lady Luck has turned back around,* he thought, as he hopped on the streetcar and headed north.

As the next months rolled by, Carlos returned to the Southland, increasing his winnings. He was relieved with the realization that, at last, he had found a way to keep his head above water, financially. He didn't come out ahead every time, but he maintained a discipline with his betting, learning to play the odds, and limiting the number of drinks he took while playing. By springtime, he had won a total of nearly four thousand bucks, and he was beginning to attract attention from the dealers and box men who ran the games for Benny Binion. Benny didn't want to be known as someone running fleece joints. He had a high-class clientele, including many of the city's prominent bankers, some actors and radio stars, and even one Dallas district attorney. H. L. Hunt, the wealthy Dallas oilman, was a valued client. However, the bulk of his customers were regulars, some who were professional gamblers, and others who were simply professionals and businessmen. He didn't want truck drivers or working stiffs, because he came from a similar background and didn't want to exploit those people.[5]

[5] *Blood Aces: The Wild Ride of Benny Binion, the Texas Gangster Who Created Vegas Poker,* by Doug J. Swanson, published by Viking, an imprint of Penguin Publishing Group, a division of Penguin Random House LLC. Copyright © 2014 by Doug J. Swanson

CHAPTER TWENTY-SIX

DECEMBER 1944—DALLAS

One night, Carlos had stopped by a downtown bar after work, and after a few drinks, he decided to hit the Southland again. Finding a spot at the table, he pulled out his roll of gambling money, bought some chips, and ordered a drink from the cocktail waitress. He was feeling no pain, great in fact, and was confident of another good night at the tables. When it was his first turn as a shooter, he rolled an eight. As he shook the ivories a second time, he said to himself, "Come on, eighter from Decatur!" and tossed them against the back wall. Sure enough, he got a five and a three, and everyone cheered him on. He was doing well and kept drinking and betting larger and larger stacks of chips. But at last, the inevitable happened, and he lost all his winnings on a snake-eyes tossed by some clod-hopper beanpole down at the other end of the table. Carlos was furious! "You goddam son of a bitch!" he yelled. Then he swore at the stickman, "And you moved my chips, goddam you!" The others at the table were stunned, but Carlos kept ranting about being cheated, and how the game was crooked, with shills and loaded dice. Two bouncers quickly moved in on him. He tried to throw a punch, but one of the men swiveled quickly and landed one in Carlos's gut. The two of them then grabbed Carlos and took him out the door, down the back stairs and out to the alley, where they punched and kicked him unmercifully, leaving him battered and bloody, stuffed in a putrid-smelling garbage can.

Carlos wasn't the only one who was furious. When the boxman went to Benny's office and told him what transpired, Benny went bananas. "Goddamn it! How could you dumbasses let this happen! Do you know that Don Ameche is coming later tonight? I got a goddamned movie star, one of my top customers, coming to play craps in a few minutes, and all he's going to hear is how some asshole sumbitch accused me of running a crooked game!" Then, as he cooled down, Benny said, "I hope you had Tweedle Dee and Tweedle Dum blow this joker's head off!" When he learned that hadn't happened, Benny went into a second hissy fit. It was only the next day, after Ameche had come and gone, that he began to make his plan.

First of all, he had to find out who the fat little bastard was. The next morning, after stewing over his breakfast, he assembled all his employees at the Southland. "Boys and girls," he said, "I guess everybody knows what happened last night. This asshole got drunk and accused us of running a crooked game, kicked up a hell of a ruckus, and got his ass escorted out the back way. I need to find him and give him a token of my affection. Does anybody here know who the bastard is?" A couple of dealers raised their hands tentatively.

"I don't know much about him, but he comes in from time to time. He usually bets pretty careful, and watches the booze, but last night was a doozy. I think his first name is Carl or Carlos, but I don't know his last name."

On hearing this, Nick's cousin Tony raised his hand and said, "Boss, I got an idea. Can we talk in private?"

"Okay, the rest of you scram." Once Benny was alone with Tony, he said, "Okay, whadda you got?"

"I didn't want to say nothing in front of all the others, because it involves one of my relatives, who's not involved in this thing that happened. But my cousin is the one who arranged for this guy to come here the first time. I don't know the guy, but I'm pretty sure I can find out his name and more about him."

Benny said, "You shoulda been more careful about who you let into my place, but I'll overlook that if you can find out more about this guy. I wanna know everything about him. His name, where he lives, who he works for, the kind of car he drives, his dog's name, who he's married to, the works."

CHAPTER TWENTY-SEVEN

A SUMMER EVENING IN 1945—DALLAS

Doris woke up, startled and shaking, her heart racing. She had that dream again, so real in every detail. She reviewed it in her mind, trying at the same time to submerge it. It was a day she and Carlos went at it again. As evening came, Doris had decided she should go back to see if he had woken and sobered up, or if he was still passed out. She stepped back into the house carefully, peeked through the kitchen, and saw him still there, at the table, with a nearly empty bottle beside him. He was asleep, so she put her things down in the entryway and went to the bathroom. As she was combing her hair, she heard an enormous roar from the other room: "Where the hell have you BEEN!" Terrified, she realized he must have seen her gloves and purse by the door. He was thumping around, bumping into furniture, yelling incoherently. She was really frightened and wasn't about to go back out there.

After about five minutes, which seemed like an hour, it grew quiet. She began to think she might go to the kitchen—she was hungry and needed to get something quick from the icebox so she could keep her strength. But she was terrified. What if he was waiting for her? What if he was going to attack her, like he threatened to do a week or so ago? How could she defend herself?

She knew he kept his gun in his sock drawer. She had found it there when she was putting up the laundry and saw the box of cartridges too. She opened the drawer, found the pistol, and took the box of shells. She sat down on the bed and loaded every chamber, calm in her deliberation, and then stood up, and let the pistol hang by her side. It was cold and heavy, much heavier than she imagined, and it filled her with dread. But she also felt a sense of peace, knowing that she could protect herself if need be.

She went quietly down the hall, around through the dining room, and looked in the kitchen. He was sitting at the breakfast table, drinking from a marmalade jar. She hesitated, and then walked in. Surprisingly, he seemed calm. "Where you been?" he asked.

"I was just out getting some groceries and then dropped by Sophie's," she said, shaking as she answered, the gun hidden behind her skirt.

"Well, I'm hungry; let's have some grub," he said.

She moved over to a small counter and slid the gun under a towel while he looked at his glass.

"Okay, Carlos, I'll fry some eggs and we've got some ham too," she said, as she moved toward the stove.

He was quiet, then he said, "I know where you been, you god-damned slut!" Her heart sank, as she saw where this was going. He tried to rise from the table, and as he lifted from the chair, his left arm knocked the whiskey bottle over. He grabbed it as it fell and continued to swivel up and to the right, the bottle swinging toward her face. But she was quicker. She reached over to the countertop, under the towel, and grasped the gun by the handle. Overweight, he was not well-coordinated, and his feet got entangled in the chair, just as she swung the gun in an arc from right to left. Without aiming, without thinking, she fired into his right temple, bringing him down like a sack of potatoes.

Black clouds of starlings erupted from the trees as the shot rang out through the open kitchen window, and Doris woke up shaking, muscles tensed, heart racing. She looked over and saw an empty space where Carlos usually lay sprawled on the bed, snoring. "What a terrible nightmare," she said to herself. *It felt so real! I've got to get over him; he's driving me crazy! I can't feel normal anymore*, she thought. It was hours later before she finally drifted back asleep.

CHAPTER TWENTY-EIGHT

JUNE 2, 1945—DALLAS

Although night had fallen, it was still quite warm, the heat of the day still baking from the walls of their most recent home, which felt like an imperceptibly cooling oven, although it was only May. Doris didn't think about the heat, didn't even hope for the slight breeze that often rose slowly from the south windows in front. In fact, she was chilled, the hairs on her bare arms rising and a strange sheen of moisture on her skin.

It had been a sunny, steamy, nasty day. This fight had started soon after breakfast, when she mentioned getting together with some of her sorority friends to celebrate her birthday. He was withering in his reproaches, snarling about her "uppity" friends, their snotty husbands, their airs, their cars, their beautiful children. She was indignant—they were her cherished pals from her past life, and they warmed her thoughts—a welcome relief from the cold terror that had crept into their life together. The early quarrel turned bad, more serious with attacks about her character, her role as a wife, as a partner. He had grown morose about work, about losing his job, his bad luck, and took his disappointment out on her. He didn't acknowledge how she contributed, how hard she worked, and how her income was helping them pay the bills. Instead, he seemed to feel that she was somehow sneering at his efforts, that despite her patience with his many career disappointments, that she was at fault, that she was the cause of all their problems.

The fights had gotten so much worse. His drinking made them almost unbearable for her. As he drank, he first became maudlin, and then fell into this horrible spiral of contempt, of abuse, and of hatred. She couldn't reason with him when he got this way; his fury was palpable. The least little thing would set him off—a mention of a conversation with a girlfriend, a bill from the light company or the department stores, being a few minutes late coming home after staying late at work—it was all so unreasonable.

The first time he hit her she was so shocked she couldn't even react. Nobody had ever struck her before. She didn't know what to make of it. She thought at first that she deserved it, but as she thought about the incident, she realized that she had not done anything wrong; she had simply been honest about forgetting to mail the check to the bank. The next time, it was because she objected to going out one night when she was very tired after a heavy day at work. She'd tried to be careful of his feelings, but he just blew up. It was starting to feel like her nightmare, that she was having almost every night.

CHAPTER TWENTY-NINE

COMING HOME—DALLAS AND ADA

There were so many things, so many fights. so many arguments about nothing. About nothing! And then Sunday, he had sat there drinking all day. He started in the morning after their argument Saturday night. He was quiet, just sat there drinking. She asked him if he didn't want to eat, and he didn't reply. He got up, staggered into the bathroom, came back, and drank more. Then he got up and got another bottle. By afternoon, he had passed out. She was glad. She went out to the corner store up the street and picked up a few groceries they needed to start the week out. But once she was out, she didn't want to go back. If he was still asleep, it would be a depressing reminder of how they had spent so many of the last weekends, but if he was awake, she was certain that the fights would start again. It was her nightmare all over again. So, she called Sophie and made plans to go to a movie downtown. She needed someone else to talk to, someone else to get her mind off all this.

He was still sweating; it was an uncomfortable night. Carlos had gotten up late on Sunday after a Saturday night of heavy boozing, and he had a terrific headache. He didn't think he could keep any food down, and he wasn't hungry anyway. His heart was racing, and his hands shook. The only thing that might calm him down, he thought, was "the hair of the dog." He took his first shot at 9:00 a.m. Doris had left to go to church, and he tried to read the Sunday funnies, but he couldn't concentrate. As the day wore on, he continued to drink. He got up occasionally to turn up the radio and go to the bathroom, but he always came back to the breakfast room and sat back down at the round oak table. By mid-afternoon, he was in bad shape. When Doris came back from church she had launched into a big lecture about his drinking, then about how he couldn't keep a job, and then about his sour mood and mean comments about her. Before he knew it, he had hauled off and slugged her, and she ran out of the house crying. He was ashamed of himself, not least because most of what she had said was true, and he hated hearing it from her. His head was spinning; the room was spinning. He took another drink, got up, and went to the bedroom. He opened the upper right drawer of his dresser. Then he went back to the breakfast area.

Soon, it was early evening, twilight, and the light shone above the table where he sat. There was a slight breeze through the venetian blinds from the open window, and the sound of crickets, outside.

Carlos closed his eyes and swallowed. His mouth was dry and felt full of sour cotton, or a dirty sock. He lifted his right hand, feeling the cold weight. He thought about Mother, so burdened by his father's death, all alone for so long. He remembered good times—like the time that he and Ed were jumping through a burning pile of leaves, the afternoon before the circus. Ed's feet were so burned they had to take him to the show in a borrowed baby buggy. He thought about his brothers and sisters, his cousins, and how he loved them all, how he missed them all, and especially his father. How he wished they could sit on the porch swing together again, and that he could open his heart, and ask him to explain it all in his calm, steady voice. But Lady Luck had abandoned him—just like all the other women in his life.

There was a whirring noise, a sense of something or someone in the room, his vision swirling, and his ears suddenly began ringing. The light expanded, then almost blacked out and then exploded.

In his last seconds, he was suddenly riding his bicycle, and it was a bright sunny day, just a few puffy white clouds in the light blue sky. The air was just right as it washed over his face, fluttered his shirt and the streamers on his handlebars. He wheeled by the shops, the drugstore, and the blacksmith, and the dogs came out to bark and run after him for some distance before giving up as they always did, and he smiled as the little brown spotted one dropped off last. He pushed on, under the shade trees, past the neighbor cutting his grass, up onto the footpath, and back off again when it gave out, getting closer. The last block, and he cut across a neighbor's yard and through an opening in the fence behind. The wheels bounced, the handles hard and shiny before him. His heart was beating stronger. Now, it was urgent, and he felt he had to push harder. *Father, I'm coming home,* he thought. And then, he was there.

CHAPTER THIRTY

JUNE 10, 1945—ADA, OKLAHOMA

The funeral was held a week later, in Ada. It was such a small town it was possible to walk to almost any destination, under the dappled shade of tree-lined walks. A soft light poured through the funeral parlor window, and there was a strong smell of flowers, which barely masked that of wax and decay. Carlos lay in an open rich wood coffin, lined with creamy quilted satin. He was dressed in a gabardine suit, and the only indication of the cause of his death was the dark brown patches under his eyes. He looked like he might suddenly wake up and dash off to a business meeting. There were candles, white gladiolas, the soft sounds of weeping, the whispered conversations, and the people—neighbors, relatives, and friends of the family in their somber Sunday best. Afterward, two women wrapped in streaks of dark clothing hurriedly swept from his mother's home, unsmiling and unspeaking, anxious to be anywhere else.

CHAPTER THIRTY-ONE

MONDAY, MAY 21, 1945—DALLAS

A few weeks before, Benny had been seated in the diner when Nick's cousin Tony came in. Benny beckoned to him and nodded at the banquette, opposite. "All right," Benny said, "whaddya you got?"

Tony said, "Well, I've already told you his name, where he lives, where he works, and all that stuff. I also told you that he's married. But what I just learned is that they have big marriage problems. It's probably mostly about money, that's where marriage problems usually start. But it's gotten bad. He gets drunk, beats her up, and messes with her head. He's twenty years older than her, and she calls him an old sot who can't get it up, and that makes him blow his top. They're at each other tooth and nail almost every minute they're together. He's lost several jobs, and now works commission only. She's a secretary at some insurance company, and between the two of them, they live beyond their means."

Benny said, "So what does all that have to do with anything?"

"Here's my idea, Boss. Let me talk to her and pitch her a deal. I'll tell her that we're a finance agency that's lost a lot of money on him, and we've tried everything to get him to stay still for a minute so we can negotiate with him, but he keeps avoiding us. All we want is for her to arrange for us to talk to him alone and quietly sometime soon. We know we're going to lose some money on the deal, but we just want to negotiate a way to cut our losses. And for that we're willing to offer her some money in return for helping us. It would be better, and less embarrassing for him, if we can see him at home some time when she's not there, and when he's relaxed and off his guard."

"Yeah, so what then? I don't want to talk to him; I want to blow his brains out!"

"And that's what we're going to do, Boss! I'll get her to let us have a situation where we can do that safely, so no one knows what really happened. It'll look like an accident or a suicide, no problem."

"What if she comes back at us afterward, or goes to the cops?"

"How could she? We would make it clear to her that she'd be implicated, as an accessory or even a co-conspirator. I tell you, Boss, it's foolproof. We can get this done, and even though it may look to the outside world like we're not involved, everybody will get the message, not to mess with Benny Binion."

CHAPTER THIRTY-TWO

WEDNESDAY, MAY 23, 1945—DALLAS

"Okay, Boss, it's all set up. She accepted a grand as a down payment, and I told her we'll give her another two afterward. Like we figured, she just wants the money to buy stuff she can't afford on her secretary salary. So, she's going to leave the house in the afternoon, meet with our guy, and tell him what's going on at the house. She'll leave a key under a flowerpot outside the back door, and once it's dark enough, our guy will slip in and do the deed. Once he's finished, he'll come back and report to you how it went. We've set it up for Sunday, June third. That's all there is to it. Easy-peasey."

"Okay, you done good here. There'll be a nice little bonus for you in your next check. Fingers crossed."

CHAPTER THIRTY-THREE

JUNE 3, 1945, 9:15 P.M., CWT—DALLAS

Benny put down his drink and looked at Little Johnny as he came to the doorway. "Is it done?"

"Yeah," said Johnny.

"You sure?"

"Yeah, I got him and set it up like we said: sitting down, liquor bottle, glass knocked over, and the pistol by his hand."

"Did anyone see you?" asked Benny.

"Naw, there wasn't nobody around, and I just let myself out and walked down the driveway back to the street," said Johnny.

"How about cops?"

"There wasn't any around, and I just walked down the street clear. No neighbors buzzin' around neither."

"Okay, Johnny, you done good. Tell me, is there somethin' I can do for you?"

Little Johnny scratched his chin and said, "I guess if I had enough moolah, I'd like to find myself a little restaurant and go into business."

Benny answered, "That's good to know; I'll look into it for you. I got some Dago friends in the restaurant business, and I can ask them about opportunities. Now git yourself somethin' to drink, and let's see if the coppers pick up anything."

"Yeah, okay," said Johnny.

Benny turned around and said to the tall fellow sitting next to him, "That'll teach the little shit to screw with me, Tony."

CHAPTER THIRTY-FOUR

JUNE 4, 1945 12:45 A.M., CWT—DALLAS

"Jesus!" said Doris. She was so tired she couldn't sleep, and so stressed out; it was the most stressful day she could remember. It had gone okay, she had answered all the questions and she felt that the police and the justice of the peace were satisfied with all her answers, but she was wrung out with nervous worry that it would go well. She took off her dress but fell in a heap on the bed and slept in her slip until later that night, when she woke up with terrible dreams.

"Calm down," she told herself, "Everything will be all right, but you just have to go through the next days as normally as possible." Eventually, she drifted back off to a fitful doze and woke at seven the next morning, got ready, and left for work.

CHAPTER THIRTY-FIVE

APRIL 5, 1947, 4:45 P.M.—DALLAS

"Hello, Mr. Manno?

"Yeah, this is Tony Manno. Who's calling, please?"

"You may remember me, Mr. Manno, we met about two years ago. I was married at the time to a man named Carlos."

"Yeah, I remember you, and I remember what we did for you back then."

"Well then, you won't find it strange that I want to ask for some more help. The help that you gave me then didn't last very long, and I need some additional assistance."

"You gotta be kiddin' me, lady. You got all the help you asked for and all the help you're gonna get, and the whole matter is over and done with."

"Not quite, Mr. Manno, it seems that a certain attorney is looking into the matter and has uncovered some new information that could affect you and your client."

"Whadda you mean, my client? I ain't got no client."

"That's not what this attorney says. He says he has information that could make things very sticky for both of you. And of course, I haven't said anything to him. Yet."

"Listen, we can't talk about this over the phone; this is just crazy! We gotta meet and get you set straight."

"I agree, we should meet, together with my lawyer. We can talk freely, he can tell you what he knows, and everything that's said will be privileged so it can't be used in court." This was something she had learned in her work at the insurance agency.

The meeting took place three days later in a downtown office building. Doris made sure Manno came alone, as she insisted, before appearing, herself. Manno knocked on the office door, and a tall, burly man opened it. "Mr. Manno?"

"Yeah, I'm Manno" he said, looking around. "Where's the dame?"

"Right behind you, Mr. Manno," said Doris as she followed him inside.

"Mr. Manno, I'm Charles Ford, of Ford, Jackson, and Dickens. Here's my card. Why don't you have a seat?" the attorney said, pointing to the chairs on one side of a walnut conference table. The attorney and Doris took seats opposite.

During the discussion, Manno insisted that Doris would get no further payments. Doris responded that she never understood that Carlos would be murdered but rather that her assistance would allow them to confront him and negotiate. Manno replied that she must have known because she took the second payment. She denied it and said that the little she had gotten barely covered her expenses, and she only wanted to make one more request. If they could reach agreement on a sum, she would sign a letter describing her role in Carlos's death, how she had left Carlos alone that afternoon, how she had left the key to the back door where she told him, how she stayed away until 8:00 p.m., and covered up with the justice of the peace. That letter would be left with the lawyer, with instructions to release it if she ever asked for more money or snitched on Manno and his client.

Manno objected to the use of the word client. The attorney cleared his throat and said, "Perhaps you're right; the correct term would be 'your boss.' We know you were working for Benny Binion, and you arranged everything on his behalf. This lady here is a personal friend, and I've offered to do whatever I can to help her. That includes going to the authorities with a complete description of your involvement and that of Mr. Binion, if necessary. I think Mr. Binion wouldn't be too happy with you if word of this affair gets out, and his involvement in it. I'm aware of what has happened to others who disappointed Mr. Binion, and I wouldn't want to be in your shoes if that were to occur."

Manno twisted in his chair, turned to Doris, and said, "Okay, whadda you have in mind?"

Doris calmly replied, "I'm not going to try to bleed you dry, Mr. Manno. I'll be satisfied with a one-time payment of $30,000."

"Thirty grand! That's enough to buy a mansion! You gotta be out-ta your mind!" Manno exploded.

The attorney spoke again. "Mr. Manno, I know the kind of money your boss makes. It's several million dollars a year. What my client has proposed is very reasonable, and I suggest you'd be wise to take her up on it before she raises the number."

"You can say what you wanna say, but who would believe you? There's no proof and it would just be her word against mine."

"The attorney spoke again. "Mr. Manno, you probably aren't familiar with this , but there's a new machine that records conversations. We use it for depositions." With that he rose and pushed a button on the machine on a shelf behind him. A clear recording of their discussion played until the attorney stopped and restarted the machine.

Manno was sweating by this time. "Look, I can't go to my boss with this; he'd kill me. That means it's gotta come outta my own pocket. I ain't no Benny Binion," he said. "I don't have that kind of dough just lyin' around. You gotta believe me!"

"We understand, Mr. Manno, but you're a resourceful man," the attorney said. "I'm sure you can arrange something."

"What about 10 g's a year for three years?" asked Manno.

The attorney countered, "I'm afraid not, Mr. Manno. You're in a dangerous line of business, and your future is, shall we say, rather uncertain. No, I'm afraid we'll have to insist on one payment, only."

"Okay, okay," said Manno. "But you gotta give me some time to get it together."

Manno left the office, and Doris turned to her brother. "Jay, that went perfectly! You were so convincing. I can't thank you enough!"

Her brother replied, "Dee-Dee, it was risky, but I think it worked out okay. Thank your lawyer friend for letting us use his office and his tape recording machine, will you?"

CHAPTER THIRTY-SIX

1945 TO 1961—DALLAS

After Carlos's death, Doris continued her work as a secretary and was active in sorority affairs. She entertained at home, hosting teas and socials. Later, she sold the house on Rosedale and moved to the "uber-chic" Elmwood area of southwest Dallas. The very modest three bedroom-two bath home was built in 1938 and was relatively new. In 1947, she remarried, to an Army Air Corps veteran named E. Maddox Leath. He and his twin brother, Hubert Maddox Leath, were born in Oklahoma in 1919, and she was happy with his background. He was slightly less than two years younger than Doris, which was quite a change for her after Carlos, who had been two decades older. More importantly, he was only a social drinker. At the time Doris and Leath were married, he was an accountant at a landscape firm.

Later, upon her death in 1961 at age forty-four, she and her husband resided on the outer edges of the "Park Cities," exclusive, close-in independent municipalities surrounded by the Dallas city limits and near the prestigious Preston Hollow neighborhood in north Dallas. The location was so near that "University Park" was first entered as the location of the residence on her death certificate, only to be scratched out and "Dallas" later written in by hand. Leath would later take the position as a buyer for a lighting fixture supply company. Even had Doris continued working as a secretary, it's not easy to imagine the two enjoying such comfortable circumstances. Is it possible that the death of Carlos played some role?

CHAPTER THIRTY-SEVEN

JANUARY 12, 1963—DALLAS

Lew Sterrett was serving as the Dallas County Justice of the Peace at the time of Carlos's death, and it was he who responded to the report of his suicide on the evening of June 3, 1945. He went to the home in University Park, having been alerted by the Park Cities police. When he arrived, he was met at the door by the young widow, Doris. She had behaved like anyone would, displaying signs of shock, struggling to contain her emotions. He saw no reason to doubt her story. The evidence seemed clear; he saw the body and the gun, the liquor bottle, and he confirmed everything with the police detective on the scene. He saw no reason not to rule the death a suicide.

It was only after the later arrest of "Little Johnny" Brazil on charges of embezzlement that he got word that the small-time hoodlum had made explosive allegations in an effort to strike a plea deal. The gangster asserted that he knew of killings that were ordered on behalf of some gambling kingpins, including one that was staged to look like a suicide. Going back over the cases on which he had served, there were just two that occurred in the time period Little Johnny had mentioned, and one of those was the death of Don Carlos. He had always thought there might be something funny about that one; first of all, the guy's name. Although his last name didn't sound Italian, he wondered about his identification as a "don," like a mobster. But now, there was this new uncertainty, so Sterrett considered reopening the inquest.

The problem was, the gambling operations in Dallas had been cleaned up, and most of the bad guys had moved out of state, beyond the reach of the county JP. Also, the key principals in the matter were dead—both the victim, of course, and his wife. After further questioning of Little Johnny, Sterrett still suspected that the allegation might be true, but he decided there just wasn't enough evidence to substantiate the story, and he concluded that there was a good possibility that the little gangster had invented it out of whole cloth.

Sterrett, who had served as the coroner at Carlos's death died in 1981. He was seventy-nine.

Carlos left behind a landscape strewn with wreckage. Three children whom he abandoned, multiple women who had fallen in love with him and whose lives he poisoned, Jo, the unwed mother of his only son, and a promising career in tatters. Beyond that, he shattered his mother's peace of mind; she would die within a year of his death. His siblings could not bring themselves to speak of him. The echoes of his death and destructive behavior rippled down through generations, affecting those whose lives he had barely touched. It would be many years until he became just another suicide statistic of middle-aged males who killed themselves by gunshot.

Doris often woke up with the same dream, in which she nervously prepared herself for the knock on the door.